THE
JACOBITE
REBELLION

THE JACOBITE REBELLION

PAUL ADAMS

The Book Guild Ltd

First published in Great Britain in 2018 by
The Book Guild Ltd
9 Priory Business Park
Wistow Road, Kibworth
Leicestershire, LE8 0RX
Freephone: 0800 999 2982
www.bookguild.co.uk
Email: info@bookguild.co.uk
Twitter: @bookguild

Typeset in Adobe Garamond Pro

Printed and bound in Great Britain by CPI Group (UK) Ltd, Croydon, CR0 4YY

ISBN 978 1912362 554

British Library Cataloguing in Publication Data.
A catalogue record for this book is available from the British Library.

For my dear wife Jackie
To Rosie and Jasmin
To Richard and Ian
To Gurd

Author Note

I have not been to Findhorn and I am indebted to advice from Diane (nee Macbeth) Smith (most of which was ignored) who was born and bred in Findhorn. I did go to Culloden when I was 17, staying at Nairn and travelling partly along the coast towards Findhorn.

PROLOGUE –

THE COCK CROWED

I was of course aware of my illustrious namesake, Charles Edward Stuart. As far as I knew, we merely shared a name and not a genealogical history. In fact we had very little in common; he was brought up in France and Italy and mixed with royalty, and I was brought up in Dorking and mixed with students at Guildford University, where I worked as a lecturer in Medieval & Tudor History. The earlier Charles had the evocative nickname of 'Bonnie Prince Charlie', whereas the students referred to me, if they mentioned me at all which was apparently not often, as 'Stewfart'.

I suppose I was satisfied with my life, which had a certain order and routine. My wife had not been so satisfied and had left me six months earlier. I had never understood women; I certainly had not understood my wife. But then, as she was from Estonia and had few words of English, this was not very surprising. In fact the only time I understood her was when she told me she was leaving, and then the language was mostly Anglo-Saxon expletives.

She ran off with Josef, our Polish plumber. In retrospect I should have suspected that something was amiss. It seemed that our house had more leaks than the Titanic, and which only manifested themselves when I was at work. Of course this required frequent visits from Josef with his wrench and other tools of the trade. I had always assumed that his comments reflected his poor grasp of English but, with hindsight, I think he was just taking the mick.

'Ah, Mr Charles, had to do work with cock for some time to great satisfaction,' and 'Mrs Stewarts called me out to spend 15 minutes with wench and I go home now – she has no more need.'

The last I heard they were running a pub in Swansea, presumably the 'Cock and Wench'. Wales, how very appropriate – the Land of Leeks.

So I lived alone with Lawrence the cat. Not as moody as my wife, but just as uncommunicative. Of course neither of us realised that our lives were just about to change forever, as we were drawn into a world of international mystery and intrigue.

WEDNESDAY MORNING –

THE EARLY BIRD

It all started with the dawn raid. It was not like any other dawn raid… for a start it took place at 8.30 in the morning.

Police overtime had been severely cut back following the botched police force amalgamation. The former Home Secretary had decreed that one police force would be better than two and, forgetting that the main priority of a modern police force was to harass motorists, had decided that amalgamated county forces would be better able to combat terrorists and super criminals.

Originally Surrey was to merge with Hampshire but this plan was quickly scrapped when the Chief Constable realised that he would be personally responsible for the naval ratings in Portsmouth. Terrorists and super criminals all rolled into one implacable foe. Downtown Basra would have been preferable to Portsmouth on a Friday night.

By using his considerable influence, and the police files on Surrey MPs complete with pictures of their so-called 'nieces', or on two cases their 'nephews', he was able to promote a union with Kent. With more motorways than any other proposed amalgamation, this combination would be particularly suited for the latest forward thinking – new speed cameras, sensing devices that can tell whether a driver had been smoking in a confined space, and also the correct way to herd motorway traffic into one lane when a Mini has broken down on the hard shoulder 16 miles ahead, and all required extensive study. The Chief Constable personally carried out research in the south of France, Italy and Japan. The Florida trip was only cancelled when a new Home Secretary scrapped the whole plan. This came as a surprise to everyone apart from the Chief Constable of Yorkshire who had vehemently opposed any amalgamation. But then the new Home Secretary was from Yorkshire, and the Yorkshire police had files too!

No one was charged with wasting police time.

As far as Surrey was concerned, all they had to show for the wasted expenditure was a market research document detailing what the citizens of Surrey and Kent wanted from their police force. Later known as the 'Greta Garbo Report' it found that they just wanted to be left alone.

It was not like any other dawn raid...

It was supposed to take place on a Thursday, which, apparently, was the standard day for police raids agreed with Richard Murdoch. A Thursday gave maximum opportunity for in-depth background of the raid to be prepared for the Saturday and Sunday editions.

A Thursday had duly been arranged when the editor of the *Sun* realised that there was a European Champions

League semi-final that night. Plucky English police holding terrorists after dramatic shoot-out would have to play second fiddle to plucky English team winning on penalties after dramatic shoot-out. The front page was therefore already taken. The Friday was suggested instead which still left time for the weekend editions, but the Home Office vetoed this. The new Home Secretary wanted to take credit for the raid, provided it was a success of course, but he would be out of the country on the Friday, visiting Barbados with a small team of journalists and his attractive new PR lady. He was planning to show the British public that he was ceaseless in his concern for their safety by announcing a new Anti-Terrorism Bill to coincide with the raid. He would rather not do this from the Barbados Hilton in a pair of swimming trunks.

A new bill was required urgently to clarify the inconsistencies and contradictions in the three Acts introduced by his predecessor. The courts had pointed out that conspiring with persons unknown had not been intended by Parliament to mean unknown to the conspirator, only to the police. Neither did consorting with known terrorists apply to persons who had merely been placed in the same police cell. There was also an amendment required to correct the faulty drafting of the April 2006 Act. Detention without charge had been increased to 42 days but the wording was such that the Law Lords decided that this did not include nights. The police were forced to take suspects home each day and collect them again the following morning. A source of great hilarity to the general public but seen by the tabloid newspapers as the greatest threat to our nation since the invasion of Polish plumbers. 'Police Force in Police Farce' thundered the *Daily Mail*. Something clearly had to be done.

And so the day finally settled on was the Wednesday, but turnout would be limited to the BBC, ITV News, The Times, Sky, the *Sun* and Porter, the terrorist correspondent of the *Dorking Chronicle*. It was an immense scoop for the *Chronicle* who had the only photos and eyewitness accounts of the morning's dramatic proceedings. Perhaps they would be able to make a killing on the syndication rights.

The others, used to early morning dawn raids, had not allowed for rush hour traffic and either failed to arrive on time, or in the case of the BBC, turned up late.

Blissfully unaware that I was causing so much trouble, I set out for work at 8.30 as usual. I do not know who was the more surprised when I opened the front door, myself or P.C. Harding who was just about to batter the door down. He pulled back abruptly and then, unsteady on his feet, fell back into the flower bed. Taken aback by this premature assault the remaining squad crouched down, pistols pointed menacingly at my vital organs. A number of them shouted confusing and contradictory instructions about what to do with my hands. Resembling an out-of-control semaphore or an on-course bookie, I eventually decided to put my hands on my head as I had seen in countless TV shows. This did of course mean letting go of my briefcase – stunning the unfortunate P.C. Harding who was struggling to rise to his feet, gingerly feeling his ankle as he did so.

The reporter took the opportunity to photograph Harding picking himself up from the flower bed for the second time, which later provided evidence for my alleged assault. Doubling as the *Chronicle* gardening correspondent Porter was also in the process of snapping my roses, which had an unusual shade of blue and of which I was particularly proud, when he was unceremoniously barged out of the way by the police hit team making their way up to the front door. Luckily his fall was broken by P.C. Harding – who ended up face down for the third time in as many minutes, his injuries growing.

Detective Inspector Monro surveyed the operation with the eye of an experienced professional. A textbook operation with only one casualty so far, and no fatalities, unlike last month's raid at the Manse of a certain Reverend Smythe. It was not Monro's fault that the Vicar had been wrongly identified as a dangerous Moslem fundamentalist and anyway, what person in their right mind mends table legs at 5am in the morning. The D.I. was determined to get this raid right. Fast-tracked for quick promotion in Special Branch he could not afford another disaster on his record.

The police team rushed into the house and spread out looking for other occupants. As it happened the only other occupant had, at an identical moment, entered through the back door cat flap. Lawrence was a smart cat and, quickly taking note of the number and quality of the opposition, decided not to make a last stand, instead retreating the way he had come, completely unaware that he was about to feature in the cat equivalent of *Butch Cassidy and the Sundance Kid*.

P.C. Evans was not happy. He had joined the Firearms Unit for the overtime and the extra money. But also, the shift work enabled him to plan his week like clockwork. Training on Mondays, briefings on Tuesdays, day off on Wednesdays, dawn raids on Thursdays, debrief on Fridays and the occasional VIP support duty planned well in advance. This left plenty of time for a social life, particularly Tuesdays when he would be out drinking with his mates knowing that he could sleep it off the next day. Not this Wednesday. The unexpected phone call at 5am that morning was a shock to his system. He dimly remembered being told that there was no one else available due to suspension and injury (two officers had wounded each other on a poorly lit stairway the day before). By 8.30am he could just about focus sufficiently to identify objects through his telescopic sights, provided that they were large, say... elephant size.

Hearing a commotion at the front of the house Evans trained his telescopic sights on the back door as he had done many times before. Unlike any other time before there was a sudden movement. His colleague Dickens shouted out the usual 'Police, halt' warning when the shot rang out. There was a split second between the sharp cracking sound and the realisation that he had shot a suspected cat. Even if Lawrence was mostly of Arabian stock it was hardly a reason for a quasi-judicial execution, as the subsequent enquiry confirmed. Neither was the fact that Lawrence was a noted serial killer, well known to the local bird and mouse population. Frantically searching his mind for justification the best that Evans could come up with was that the mouse in Lawrence's mouth could have looked like a gun – from a distance – in the half-light. It might have worked but perhaps not on a

6

bright spring morning like today. He sheepishly radioed D.I. Monro.

"Wicket Keeper 1 to Opening Batsman."

"Come in Wicket Keeper 1." Monro looked pleased with himself. The use of cricketing terms was, he felt, particularly stylish.

"I have made a catch behind the back door… I mean the wicket. I think it might be fatal."

"Roger. Secure the area. I will contact the backup ambulance unit."

Hearing this exchange I remonstrated with Monro, "But you can't have killed him. Lawrence would not hurt a fly, well… maybe a fly, or a mouse…"

"We'll be the judge of that Sir, my men are entitled to protect themselves."

"From a cat?"

Monro looked puzzled. "Wicket Keeper 1, please describe the casualty."

"Greyish white, about 2 feet with…"

The third casualty of the day was radio protocol as D.I. Monro began to fear the worst. "Cut the crap Evans, is it a cat?"

"Hard to tell in this light, sir."

"Dickens, is it a cat?"

"Looks like a cat to me, Gov, but it is a big one." How he thought that this would help P.C. Evans, only he could say.

Monro put his face in his hands and groaned. He would never live this down. The cheery comments in the canteen about 'Catastrophes' and 'Catalogues' of disasters. And this following the 'The Manse Murder Mystery' as the *Guardian* called it. Suddenly angry, he remembered me.

"Alright, sunshine, you've had your fun and games. Now I have to read you your rights."

"What for?"

"You are suspected of being a terrorist in contravention of the Prevention of Terrorism Act, April, 2006." This apparently augmented or superseded the Acts of January and March 2006. No one was quite sure.

"You do not have to say anything…"

"You shot my cat."

"You do not have to say anything…"

"I was fond of that cat."

"You particularly do not have to say anything about your bloody cat!" shouted Monro, wincing at the irony of this description.

"But I have not done anything!"

"They all say that at first"

"But most of them haven't according to the papers. They are usually innocent citizens like me."

"Don't believe everything you read in the papers, sunshine."

"What about that Vicar last week…"

"Look, we are not here to have a bloody debate. I'll start again. You do not have to say anything but…"

"Excuse me sir, is that your car?" The voice exuded all the authority of someone wearing a peaked cap in the line of duty.

"What?" asked Monro in a peevish tone.

"Is that you car sir? The silver Vauxhall Astra."

"Yes, but it's a police car. I'm on duty."

"Doesn't look much like a police car to me. There are

8

two proper police cars parked round the corner. Volvos, with stripes and flashing lights and everything."

Monro found the idea that he was not driving a 'proper police car' extremely irritating. "Well it's my police car, so piss off and mind your own business."

"This is my business," bridled the warden. "Are you a resident? After 8.30am you need a resident's permit to park here."

"Of course I'm not a resident."

"I'm a resident," I volunteered helpfully.

"There you are then," said peaked cap. "If you are visiting this gentleman, you could have asked him for a visitors' parking sticker."

"Are you seriously suggesting that I should have phoned up chummy and said 'Look, we are raiding your house at 8.30 tomorrow morning please could you stand outside with visitors parking stickers for me and the lads!"

The veins on Monro's forehead were beginning to throb dangerously.

"That would have been sensible sir. Forward planning makes all the difference."

Monro exploded. "Piss off before I arrest you for obstructing justice. I can take you down the nick and hold you for 24 hours without so much as a cup of tea."

"If that's your final word," said peaked cap, beating a hasty retreat. He was never happy when people did not respect the uniform. Still he was not the sort to be put off by rudeness. After all, he had been on a County Council assertiveness course. He had learnt that a tow truck could be very assertive.

"You do not have to say anything but anything that you do say may be used against you…"

" Good morning. I represent the Liberal Democrats, can I count on your support at the by-election next Thursday?"

Monro looked at me, and then at a small, thin man hiding behind a giant yellow rosette, looking for all the world like a walking sunflower. It was very clear from the look of contempt on Monro's face that declaring yourself as a Liberal Democrat is something that would definitely be used against you.

"What the hell do you want?" he said, on the verge of losing his temper. The arteries and veins on his forehead were beginning to look like an electrical wiring diagram and I couldn't help remembering the old bomb disposal films:'Whatever you do, do not cut the blue vein, he might explode.'

Unperturbed, Sunflower launched into his patter, "I am sure that I want the same as you. A country where no one is above the law, and a land where citizens can go about their lawful business without being hindered by the state. Our liberties are being steadily taken away. Did you know that…"

"I AM going about my lawful business," remonstrated Monro, "arresting villains. The only person taking liberties here is you, AND YOU…" The last part was shouted at peaked cap who was watching from the relative safety of the other side of the garden wall.

"Is that still your final word?" shouted peaked cap without receiving an answer.

"I'm supporting you lot, the Liberals."

Sunflower was pleased to hear a friendly voice, which in this case came from the local Royal Mail representative making his way up the garden path, rummaging in his postbag as he did so.

"We need to get tougher on immigrants and other criminals. We need more policeman on the streets," continued Postbag.

"Absolutely right, more police on the streets," echoed Sunflower.

Not on my street, I thought, there were at least three in the house, a sniper or two in the back garden, D.I. Monro, two uniforms standing idly by the gate leering at an attractive woman P.C. making her way past, and not forgetting P.C. Harding who was by this time limping his way up the garden path leaning on Porter, from the *Chronicle*, as support. I think that, as a taxpayer, I was certainly getting my money's worth!

Monro was now a very angry man, his textbook operation was descending into farce. "If you have some post put it through the letter box, if not piss off or I'll stick YOU through the letter box."

"I only have this parcel, but I do need a signature," he said thrusting a pad and pen in my direction.

"Don't sign anything until you have received proper professional advice."

I vaguely recognised a neighbour crossing over the small garden wall and striding purposely towards our little group, his briefcase leading the way.

"Has he read you your rights? He should read you your rights you know. Allow me to give you my card," the

Briefcase said briskly. I took the card, which identified him as a representative of 'Had an accident – Not your fault.com' with the address of a local firm of solicitors.

"Look, as much as I would like to stay and chat, I need to get on with my round," lied Postbag. Really he just wanted to put several letter boxes between himself and D.I. Monro. "I just need to deliver this parcel."

"I think that I'll take that as evidence, thank you." exclaimed Monro grabbing the parcel.

Briefcase startled me by grabbing the package back from Monro. I was very surprised and impressed that he had it in him.

"You can't take that. It's unlawful. The Postal Communications Act requires a magistrate's consent before you can tamper with the Royal Mail." Postbag and Sunflower nodded their agreement and proceeded to discuss the various legal issues with Briefcase. Sunflower was particularly vocal about stopping this latest attempt by the state to extend its surveillance of citizens without proper judicial safeguards. Briefcase kept referring to his 'client', meaning me, I suppose. I felt more and more of a bit part player in the drama unfolding around me.

"I don't need lectures on the law," screamed Monro, "I am the law."

His attempt to snatch back 'Exhibit A' was rebuffed by the trio in a deft game of pass the parcel.

Looking for help, Monro gesticulated at the approaching lady PC. "Get over here, love. And your name is? Linda. Linda, these three men will need to be restrained."

"I find that that happens a lot," she sighed.

"You know the routine."

"No complaints so far."

"Well get on with it."

"Off with it more like," she pouted, beginning to unbutton her uniform tunic.

Monro's jaw dropped in incredulity. Linda had removed her blouse by the time he recovered his composure. "What the hell do you think you are doing?"

"I'm the birthday strippergram," she announced confidently, by now waving her bra above her head theatrically. Judging from the look of astonishment on the faces of our little group she began to have doubts. "This is number 36, isn't it?"

"No," I replied. "This is number 26. You want Father O'Leary, a few doors down."

"But I saw a game of pass the parcel, and what about the three-legged race over there," she said pointing in the direction of Harding and Porter. "This must be a birthday party."

Sunflower did not know where to look. Or rather he did know where to look, he just did not want to be caught at it. He was not the only one looking for support that morning, having been joined by several prominent parts of 'PC' Linda's anatomy. The PC had turned out to be very non-PC.

"If you and your bloody friends are finished, PERHAPS WE COULD GET ON WITH THE ARREST." The pressure was becoming too much for Monro as he dabbed at a nosebleed with his handkerchief.

"Don't shout at him on his birthday," demanded Linda sympathetically.

"It's not my birthday."

"And trying to pinch his parcel. That's a rotten thing to do. Bound to be a birthday present," added Postbag.

"But it's not my birthday.. Oh forget it," I wonder if any of them would notice if I went quietly off to work.

"I insist that you read him his rights," demanded Briefcase.

"What the hell do you think I have being trying to do, sing him a selection from Gilbert & Sullivan operas?"

"'A Policeman's Lot is not a Happy One' might very well be appropriate," I ventured.

Monro scowled at me and I could see his forehead ticking dangerously.

Time to keep quiet before he did indeed explode.

"You do not have to say anything but…"

Monro did not finish the sentence as just at that moment he realised that he had not cancelled the backup medics. He caught sight of a stretcher with body bag being carried out of the front door of the house, the two medics looking furious as they walked past. They had better things to do with their time then dealing with feline fatalities. "The paperwork…" groaned Monro.

By this time the neighbours were gathering and looking at each other knowingly. All the little pieces of evidence were beginning to come together in their heads.

"He murdered his wife," said one confidently.

"I wondered what had happened to her."

"She must have been very small," said her neighbour eyeing the stretcher.

"I heard that that was all they could find of her."

"I heard that it was just her hand and a handbag."

"A handbag?" drawled another.

"Wasn't there something about a cat?"

"That's where the rest of her went. Minced up and fed to the cat!"

The 'torsoless handbag' was duly loaded onto the ambulance, which was then driven off in a welter of flashing lights and sirens. Quite why or where to remains a mystery.

"I've had enough of this. You – get in the car."

"What car?" I enquired politely.

"Don't play games, sunshine. I've had enough of your antics. You too." He called out, "Get him into the car and then disperse this crowd. I will see what's happening inside."

The two PCs propping up the gate looked sheepish.

"But Gov…"

"No buts just get on with it."

"But Gov…" they repeated pointing towards Peaked Hat. The warden had that look of self-satisfaction, which appears when you have achieved something that makes your day, or in this case his year. The silver Astra was disappearing down the road on the back of a tow truck from the Surrey Police Traffic Response Unit (motto Tough on Congestion – Tough on the Causes of Congestion.)

Deciding to look busy for once, the two PCs hurriedly proceeded with the second part of their instructions and addressed the crowd.

"Come along now, haven't you got homes to go to. There's nothing to see here."

"Nothing to see here," echoed his colleague.

The BBC camera team who had at last arrived did not agree with this observation. Neither, they thought, would the millions of viewers who would be watching the news that night. They would see Harding wincing as Porter tried to apply a home-made sling (actually Linda's bra, generously donated for the purpose). Postbag had his trouser leg rolled up, like a uniformed Mason, showing the solicitor bite marks on his leg from an earlier incident. Sunflower was trying to lead the neighbours in a chorus of 'Happy Birthday to you' while 'PC' Linda was making the most of what the media would call 'Prime Time Exposure', taking up a succession of provocative poses. Finally, they would be treated to a close-up of D.I. Monro giving the traffic warden a bit of assertiveness training that had been left out of the County Council course. Catching sight of the BBC at last, Monro let go of the warden's neck long enough to make a statement on camera. He had of course received extensive media training for just such an event.

"Oh Sh*t," was the best he could manage.

All in all it had not been an ordinary dawn raid although of course none of this appeared in Monro's report. Neither did it appear in the BBC news broadcasts. The maniacal look on the DI's face as he had tried to throttle Peaked Cap together with a renewed nosebleed turning his hands a bloody red shocked the BBC news editors. They decided that they could not show pictures of a man having his throat torn out by a policeman on national television, and scrapped the entire coverage.

***

Porter was initially disappointed about the syndication of his articles.

The next day's headlines were dominated by the latest royal scandal. For months the paparazzi had been following Jenny Berkshire, Prince Albert's so-called girlfriend, about her daily rounds. Jenny shops, Jenny meets a chum, Jenny tries to understand the rules of Polo, discovering that a chukka is not something that happens after too much Buck's Fizz. It came to light that Jenny was a paid decoy only after Prince Albert had eloped with Peter, the Gunnery Officer from HMS Windsor, Albert's latest ship.

The only articles Porter managed to sell were featured in the *Chronicle and Cat Weekly*.

All was not lost however. A *Daily Mail* journalist browsing through *Cat Weekly* on a visit to his dentist some weeks later picked up on the cat assassination story. After a statement of no comment from the Home Secretary the newspaper ran with the now famous headline 'Cat got Your Tongue, Minister.'

The following week, the Home Secretary was forced to make a statement in the House of Commons. He was used to the usual Parliamentary catcalls but was quite unprepared for the chorus of meowing that erupted from the opposition benches. The Tory Shadow Cabinet obviously could not join in this noisy display and merely resorted to sitting in a dignified row pointing out articles in *Cat Weekly* to each other. George Galway, the independent member for Bethnal East, maintained a loud purring sound throughout and was suspended for trying to curl up in the lap of the nearest lady MP. The Liberal Democrats were more restrained. They took to waving cat collars with bells whenever the Home Secretary tried to speak. Even the Speaker failed to quell the uproar. Whenever he shouted 'Order, Order' he was greeted with cries of 'Two pints of milk please,' accompanied by sounds of lapping and slurping. This cacophony became a regular feature of Commons life each time the Home Secretary appeared in the Chamber. Eventually the Prime Minister was forced to remove him in a Cabinet reshuffle later known as the 'Night of the Long Claws.'

But this was to be some time in the future.

LATER ON WEDNESDAY –

CAT AND MOUSE

It seemed like hours, but in reality it was probably only minutes. The interview room was exactly as I had seen in many TV dramas, the canteen-style table, and the canteen-style chairs. I wondered what the canteen looked like.

DI Monro walked in with a man who was clearly his superior and both sat down on the canteen chairs opposite to me. The DI seemed more relaxed now that he was on home territory. In contrast to Monro's cockney geezer style, his boss was non-communicative and far more austere. Dressed in a grey suit, with matching hair, he wore a white shirt complementing his pallid skin. If I had possessed a packet of crayons, I would have been compelled to colour him in. His eyes and complexion were so lifeless that if he turned up at a hospital during visiting hours he would have been pronounced dead on arrival.

"This interview commenced at 10.30 am on Thursday… no Wednesday, 8th April, 2007," Monro said hastily correcting himself. Dawn raids were always on a Thursday. "Present DI Monro and Detective Chief Inspector Cumberland from Special Branch, PC Walker and the suspect, Charles Stuart."

"Answer for the record. Are you Charles Stuart of 26, Fraser Road, Dorking?"

"If not, you shot the wrong cat."

Cumberland looked up from his notes. "Cat? What cat?"

"We'll come to that, sir. A diversionary tactic employed by the suspect to avoid arrest. Charles Stuart, you have been arrested under the Terrorism Act, January 2006."

"March 2006, sir," corrected PC Walker.

DCI Cumberland sighed and leaned towards the microphone for extra emphasis. "The suspect has been arrested under The Prevention of Even More Terrorism Act of April 2006. Carry on."

They would, perhaps, be easier to remember if the legislators took a leaf from the Hollywood producers' book. The acts could have distinctive names such as:

Terrorist Act 1: Terrorist Wars
Terrorist Act 2: The Home Office Strikes Back; and
Terrorist Act 3: The Return Of the Judiciary, and
so on.

After all, the Government was already well down the road of using film ideas in their media spin. 'Be afraid, be very afraid.' and 'Just when you thought it was safe to go back to the airport'.

Monro continued, "Thank you sir. Charles Stuart, you

have been arrested under The Prevention of Even More Terrorism Act of April 2006."

"On what grounds?"

"On the grounds that you have consorted with suspected terrorists, having items in your possession that could be used in a terrorist act, and whatever else we can come up with."

"What items?"

"Do you recognise this?"

"Yes, it is a street atlas."

"For the record, the suspect has identified a street atlas of London. Is this your Street Atlas? "

"I don't know, they all look the same to me. Where did it come from?"

"We found it in your car."

"Then I assume that it is mine."

"It has your fingerprints on it."

"Then it must be mine."

"So you do not deny that it is yours?"

"Why would I?"

Monro was pleased by the way he had teased this confession out of me. He looked sideways at Cumberland for approval but the DCI was doodling on his notepad what looked suspiciously like a cat lying on its back with its legs in the air. Better press on.

"May I draw your attention to page 36? I am showing the suspect the street atlas at page 36 and pointing at an area that has been ringed in pencil. Please can you explain why you have ringed Downing Street?"

The DC leaned back with his hands behind his head

with a smug look as if to say 'Get out of that one.' Although he would have said 'Get out of that one, sunshine.'

"I have not ringed Downing Street, I have ringed Westminster Abbey."

"Don't give me that, sunshine. You have ringed Downing Street. What do you think, Walker?"

The Constable pored over the map for some time before pronouncing, "I don't know Gov, Westminster Abbey is nearer the centre of the circle."

DCI Cumberland had the casting vote, although he did not exactly put it that way. Frowning at this outbreak of democracy, he simply said, "Right we have established that it is Downing Street. Carry on Monro." As he did so he wrote Downing Street on his notepad, underlined it and marked it with a star.

"Right then, why have you also written 2pm next to Downing Street? What were you planning to do to the Prime Minister?"

"2pm is a time." I protested. "It has nothing to do with the Prime Minister."

"Are you seriously expecting me to believe that you have ringed Downing Street, written down 2pm and that this is a coincidence?"

I sighed. Clearly I was dealing with the text generation. DCI Cumberland wrote down 'something to do with the PM', double underlined it and gave it two stars.

"What were you going to do to the PM?"

"For the record Detective Sergeant Constable has entered the room," intoned Cumberland as Smith handed him a note.

"Answer the question," demanded Monro.

"It was…" I was interrupted.

"PC Sargent has entered the room," said Cumberland has he was handed another piece of paper.

"It was…"

"Detective Sergeant Constable is leaving the room."

"It was…"

"PC Sargent is now leaving the room."

"Answer the question," said Monro more forcefully.

"I'm trying to but people are coming and going like a Whitehall farce!"

Cumberland was ecstatic. He wrote down 'Whitehall – Force', treble underlined it and awarded three stars. Whenever I had seen the newspaper headline 'Police Quiz Suspects' I had imagined something like University Challenge. 'I'm going to have to hurry you. Come on…come on… Nope? Then I'll throw it open to the other side.' I do not know what scoring system Cumberland was using for this particular quiz but I could only assume that three stars implied that I was doing well and would, unfortunately, qualify for the next round.

Special Branch's very own Jeremy Paxman was delighted with the way that he had dealt with the interview so far. He hoped that the DCI would put in a good word for him during the next round of promotions. Sadly he could see that Cumberland was putting a halo on his drawing of a winged cat that was clearly on its way to a cat heaven. *I need results fast*, thought Monro, and changed the line of questioning.

"Do you recognise these men? I am showing the suspect two photographs."

I looked down at images of two grim-looking men. "The pictures are not very clear. They're a bit grainy."

"This is not a photography lesson, do you recognise these two men?"

I took a closer look. They were the sort of faces that had 'guilty' written all over them, or would have been if there was room for any more tattoos. With that amount of face decoration they would not have blended in even at a Maori wedding.

"Deal," said Monro.

I thought that that this was a bit early for a plea bargain. Seeing my look of puzzlement Monro continued.

"Deal Castle."

"Ah yes," I agreed.

"So you admit to being there?"

"Yes."

"Do you admit to meeting these men?"

"Yes."

"Did they give you anything?"

"Like what?"

"A piece of paper?"

"Yes."

"What was it?"

"A ticket."

"Was there anything else?" asked Monro in exasperation.

"Yes."

"What?"

"A set of instructions."

Monro was jubilant; he had the link he was looking for. "Ah, what did the instructions say?"

"Go out of the door and turn left."

"And?"

"Descend the stairs to your left."

"And?"

"On your right you will see…"

"Was this a guide to the castle?" snapped Monro.

"Of course it was. What else did you think they gave me?"

"Don't play cat and mouse with me sunshine, it won't do you any good," said Monro angrily.

"Well it certainly didn't do Lawrence any good," I agreed.

Cumberland's ears pricked up as he stopped doodling yet another cat on his notepad. This latest one was playing a harp. "Lawrence? Who's Lawrence? Is he in custody?"

"Yes, in a manner of speaking sir," replied Monro. As he lied, the veins in his forehead protested by throbbing gently.

"Good," said Cumberland returning to his sketch.

"Why did you go and see these two men?" continued Monro.

"I didn't go to see them. I went to look at the castle. What is the significance of the two men?"

"That is for you to tell me."

I had no idea what it was he was after. I had visited the Henry VIII gun fortification at Deal as part of the research for my book on Tudor Architecture, the same reason I had met the chief historian for English Heritage in Westminster Abbey on an earlier occasion. I cast my mind back to the time of the visit. That whole afternoon was surreal. The ticket office staff were not the usual little old ladies you would expect. I was not aware that English Heritage now employed bouncers, but I was faced with two surly Glaswegians who did everything possible to stop me entering.

"We're claesed," said one.

"But the sign outside says that you are open this afternoon."

"Aye, mebbe it does. But we're claesed for repairs."

"It is an old building," said the other one helpfully. "It was built in... when was it built Jimmy?"

"Hae would I ken. I did'ne work here then. Anyhows, it needs repairing."

"I can't hear any building work," I ventured quizzically.

"It's electrical work, they're repairing the lift." Billy was very adamant about this.

"I'm not an expert but I do not recall Henry VIII installing electrical lifts into his forts."

"It was to take shells up tae the guns," replied Billy.

"Aye," said Jimmy. "Like in that film *The Guns of Navarone.*"

"They didn't have shells like that, they had cannonballs." Like Henry's cannon, I was of course being fed a load of balls!

"Well it was tae take cannon balls up tae the guns, pal," maintained Jimmy aggressively.

I decided to accept his explanation before we reached the 'Do you want to make something of it, pal?' stage, and certainly before the 'throwing over the parapet pal', stage. We settled on half price for the ticket provided that I did not venture into the keep. I walked slowly round the walls admiring the views. The place appeared to be deserted proving that Billy and Jimmy were doing an excellent job. Even the grounds and the seafront were empty, except for the two men with trench coats and binoculars. At first I thought little of it but, as I walked around the battlements, I had the distinct feeling that several pairs of eyes were focusing on my every movement. When I looked in their direction there was a quick refocusing of the glasses on the nearest seagull. I had nearly completed the circuit when a woman emerging from inside the forbidden inner sanctum barged into me. I did not get the impression that she was an electrician. She apologised with a lilting Scottish accent, "Oh excuse me, I did not think that there was anybody here."

I do not believe in love at first sight, not unless you can see into a person's soul, or at least their bank statements. She was not classically beautiful, but there was something about those sparkling green eyes, the tumbling locks of red hair and the singsong voice that could easily have made me blow a fuse. Locking the door from which she had emerged, she made her way to the exit pausing only to glance briefly at the men on the seafront. And then she was gone – out of my life.

So I told Monro about the electrical repair work to the lifts that took the cannonballs to the guns like in the film *The Guns of Navarone*. He didn't believe me.

"About your friends, what were their names?"

"They were not my friends, but one was called Billy and the other was called Jimmy. Or it might have been the other way round."

"Look, we can do a deal. If you tell me about the others, I can see that you are let off lightly."

"Which others?" I asked.

"You don't deny that there were others then?"

"I have no idea what you are talking about."

"You said 'which others', that means a sub-group of a group of others. Had you said 'what others' then that would suggest that you really did not know what I was talking about. Tell me about the woman."

"What woman?"

"At the castle – you were seen talking to a woman."

"Ah yes," I confessed. So the birdwatchers were policemen.

"So there are others. Who is she?"

"I really have no idea. Honestly."

"We already know that her name is Margaret MacDonald, and we believe that she is part of a secret Scottish organization dedicated to the overthrow of the state. Now what else can you tell me about her."

"She has lovely green eyes."

I would not say Monro turned ugly; he was already that, but he did bang the table repeatedly as he shouted, "You might have time to waste, sunshine, but I am here to do a job. You're in this up to your f*cking neck. You admit to knowing the woman, you can't deny that. And we have the parcel, the one that you did not want me to see this morning. I am now showing the suspect an unwrapped parcel containing a book entitled 1001 *Tartans You Must See Before You Die*. What is the significance of the book? And don't try and be clever."

He did indeed show me a book with that title. I had no idea why anyone would send me such a book. In fact

28

I could not understand why anyone would want to print such a book. There are a number of these on the market such as *1001 Movies You Must See Before You Die*, or 1*001 Things You Must Do Before You Die.* They conjured up in my mind absurd medical scenes: 'No anaesthetic during surgery Doc, just wheel in a television – there is a Jean Luc Goddard film on BBC 2 that I must see.' Or 'I don't have time for an operation. Just fill up a bath with some water and fetch a dolphin – I need a swim.' In fact the most useful things to do before you die were, to the best of my knowledge, completely omitted from these guides. I have searched in vain for hints on such obvious points as making a will, calling an ambulance, or seeking a second medical opinion. I could find no guidance at all on such matters as handing over your wallet if the mugger has a knife. And the guides are completely silent on the subject of impending nuclear Armageddon heralded by a four-minute warning.

"I have absolutely no idea. I have never seen the book before in my life," I responded truthfully.

Monro continued, "Some of the tartans have been marked with a star. We think that it might be some kind of codebook. Can you explain?"

I could not.

"It is signed inside the front cover 'Love from Scheherazade.' Who is Scheherazade? What is your connection with this person?" demanded Monro.

I was dumbstruck, and hoped that it did not show. For once I had some information that Monro did not. A few days earlier I had received a postcard that had me completely baffled. The message read:

> Weather is good,
> no need for Macs
> The first letter will tell you everything
> love
> Sheherazade

I had no idea what it meant and, assuming that it was a practical joke, had thrown the card away. What was I to do, tell the truth and become more deeply involved? I decided to tell the truth. "Scheherazade is a character from the *Arabian Nights*." There I had said it; this limited disclosure was certainly true. In the fabled stories Scheherazade was the daughter of a vizier in the 9th century who married a Persian king. The king married a new virgin every night and had each one executed in the morning, a practice that I feel should have been extended to Estonian women, apart from the virgin bit obviously. By starting to tell a different tall story each night for 1001 nights, Scherezade so enchanted the king that she was to be the only wife to live. She may have written a book *1001 Tall Stories To Tell Before You Die*. In fact she probably invented the whole 1001 genre. The king would have done us all a favour if he had executed her after the very first tall chapter of the very first tall story.

"A character from Arabia," said Cumberland simultaneously writing this down in his notebook, and adding 'possible links to Al Qaeda'. "So to sum up, we have a Scottish terrorist organisation, with possible links to Al Qaeda, and a plot to assassinate the Prime Minister. And we still haven't interviewed that chap Lawrence. A good morning's work Monro." Cumberland looked at his watch. "Time for some lunch," he declared. "Interview suspended at 11.30am."

I had heard that they were known as 'Special Brunch' with good reason.

"Shall I send some food in for the suspect?" asked PC Walker.

"I suppose so, but be careful. We do not want to be accused of police brutality, or inhuman treatment."

They all trooped out laughing. Walker returned 10 minutes later with a sandwich and a lukewarm cup of tea. The sandwich could not be easily classed as either white or brown, more of a light cardboard colour, which was appropriate given the texture and the taste. The cucumber inside was fit to tile a bathroom and was almost indistinguishable in colour from the ham. I decided that Cumberland and Monro had not been joking after all, and to skip lunch. I noticed that the corner of the sandwich was curling up with a faint sneer. It was as if Monro had never left the room.

I had taken an instant dislike to Monro from our very first meeting, and with some justification. As I left for work this morning, my only contact with the Arab world was a cat called Lawrence. After meeting Monro, I had been unmasked as an international terrorist – from cat lover to Carlos the Jackal in the space of a morning. What revelations were to come this afternoon? Was I the Mafia Capo for the whole of the South of England without realising it? And what of the so-called 'codebook'? 'No need for Macs' was obviously a clue. Mackintosh with no Mac would be 'kintosh'. What then? 'First letter explains everything'. For 'kintosh' that would be a 'K'. Of course! Different tartans would be marked to indicate different letters. McBride would be a 'B' and so on. The message could then be sent by a sequence of different tartans. Difficult to crack as more than one tartan could be used to represent each letter, Macadam and McAllister, for instance, could both represent the letter 'A'. Ingenious! But why was it sent to me? Presumably someone, and I don't know who, was sending me a message by marking pages in the book.

The time passed slowly. I had nothing to do except look at the sneering sandwich of indeterminate parentage. I fancied that I could probably tell the time by the rate of curl of the sandwich. Given that it was probably made this morning, I estimated that it was after 3pm when Monro and Cumberland returned.

Monro restarted the proceedings, "Interview recommenced at 3.10pm."

I smiled at the thought that my calculation of the time was spot on.

"This is no laughing matter," exclaimed Monro. "While you've been having a leisurely lunch we have been working. We've checked your DNA and we know for instance that you have got form as a prostitute."

"Are you suggesting that I am a male prostitute?"

"No, not a male prostitute. You were arrested last year in Grimsby for street walking. We know that…" he faltered with a sudden lack of confidence. "Walker, are you sure that it was the suspect's DNA we tested?"

"You know what the desk sergeant is like, gov, especially after lunch." His hands acted out the motion of drinking. "I think he had a rush on and became confused. Fifteen school kids were brought in for suspected littering and, as no one would own up, he cautioned them all and took DNA samples for the National Database."

Cumberland coughed and looked embarrassed. "Perhaps we should come back when we have cleared this matter up, interview suspended at 3.20pm."

It was another hour or so before they returned. Again they all trooped in and took up their normal stations. Walker leaned against the wall, Monro sitting opposite me, and with Cumberland doodling away alongside him. I noticed that the latest cat had a black and white tea towel on its head and carried a cartoon-style fizzing bomb.

As previously, Monro commenced the proceedings. "We've checked out your fingerprints, Sunshine. It appears that you've form for robbery with violence."

"Really?" I enquired, "when was that?"

"Playing games again are we? You were involved in, now let me see… in…" he said, opening the file and reading the report with increasing incredulity, "in… the Great Train Robbery!!"

I burst out laughing. "I remember now. A gang of us took the morning off from nursery school!"

Monro picked up the phone. "Hawkins, I want to see the desk sergeant in 10 minutes. Well wake him up then! Interview suspended at 4.45pm."

Monro had gone a bright red.

I had been thinking that perhaps I should contact

a solicitor, particularly as I could now be charged for withholding the evidence about the codebook. I had remembered the card given to me by Briefcase of Briefcase, Sue and Billem, or whatever, and I announced, "I believe that I am entitled to phone a solicitor."

"Ah, so you need a lawyer, always a sign of guilt – so you have something to hide?" exclaimed Monro with glee. "You can use this phone here, I have to see a man about a file anyway." Cumberland looked agitated as he also left the room in a hurry. A subtle shade of pink had diffused into his cheeks and with his long, thin legs and neck he reminded me of an angry flamingo. I tried not to feel sorry for the Desk Sergeant who was to be the subject of their next interview.

The lady answering the phone at Briefcase, Sue and Billem had obviously been to the training college reserved exclusively for the future receptionists of doctors and solicitors. Occasionally RAF pilots are also sent there for courses on how to withhold information under interrogation. Reluctant to admit that anyone was in the office, let alone that there was anyone who could actually speak to me, she eventually conceded, after much arguing, that Briefcase did exist, that he did have a telephone on his desk, and that with the wonders of modern telecommunications technology it was just possible that she might be able to transfer my call. I felt a little guilty as she broke down in tears, her sobbing continuing quietly while she put me through to Briefcase. It was no doubt the imminent prospect of compulsory retraining at a secretarial Gulag that was causing her such distress.

Briefcase listened to my story impatiently, clearly annoyed at having been interrupted.

"I can't get down there this afternoon. I am very busy," he protested. "I have a PC who is claiming injury though lack of training, and who is taking advantage of our 'Two sprains for the price of one,' introductory offer. I am also representing a traffic warden who is claiming assault by the police."

These cases sounded familiar.

"And I am defending a delightful young lady who is on a charge of lewd behaviour and indecent exposure. It has taken quite a while to examine her evidence closely. I still have to recheck in detail the photos of the alleged crime, as there are a couple of interesting features in the case that require further study. All in all, you can see that I am quite busy."

The penny dropped. "But if I had not been arrested this morning you would not have any of this work."

"A fair point," he concluded. "Perhaps I could give you some introductory commission. Anyway, I have got to be in Guildford at 5.45pm to see the Bishop who has just been arrested."

"What have they arrested him for? Is he an alleged terrorist as well?"

"No, of course not. He has been arrested under the new Religious Crimes Act. The Government thought it only fair to balance up the religious hate laws with one against stirring up religious apathy. The Church of England is very worried about it. Three bishops and thirty-seven other clergy have so far been arrested. The Archbishop of Canterbury is introducing a whole raft of new measures as a matter of urgency."

"What new measures?" I asked.

"Scratch cards are bringing in the crowds. Anyone whose card reveals the number of the first hymn wins £25. Then they have teamed up with William Hill to provide odds on the length of each Sunday Service. That has proved quite controversial. Some clergy have been taking advantage by fixing the odds, and there have been undignified scenes of little old ladies being herded up the aisles, shouted at for not moving fast enough. And of vicars reading through their sermon at incredible speeds, like voice-over warnings on financial services adverts."

"But there is also the Waitrose Wine Tasting initiative. This has transformed communion in some churches, and is also a lucrative revenue stream for the Church Commissioners. You have probably seen the TV show *Vicars and Vineyards*; the best wine to drink on the second Sunday after Epiphany and that sort of thing. I think that there is to be a book tie-in. I believe also that one wine warehouse is even thinking of applying to be registered as an official place of worship. This will all help the Bishop's defence."

"This is all very fascinating, but not of much help to me."

"Look Mr. Stuart, it's nearly 5.15pm now and the police will have to take you home at 5.30pm anyway. They are not allowed to keep you overnight. So it's just a matter of refusing to say anything more today, and I can get there tomorrow morning to help you out. I made some enquiries this morning have found that the raid was by a Special Branch team dedicated to Anti-Scottish Terrorism; known in police circles as the 'Rabbie Burns Unit'."

"Then it's serious?"

"I think that you're becoming confused. The 'Serious Burns Unit' is part of the NHS. I had better go now so I'll see you tomorrow." And with that the phone went dead.

Stirring up religious apathy! That was the whole point of the Church of England. Fundamentalism and religion are the cause of many of the ills facing this country, from the Prime Minister downwards.

Briefcase was right, and I saw no more of Monro or Cumberland that day.

WEDNESDAY NIGHT –

A GAME OF TAG

I was taken down to an area of the police station they called 'The Checkout' for tagging and despatching. The name clearly came from the fact that the collection and return of suspects each day was sub-contracted to Tesco's Home Delivery service, the company that had put in the most competitive bid. There was some inconvenience to the suspects who, depending on the level of business, were expected to help unload the vehicle at various drop points before finally arriving at their own home. Still, it saved the taxpayer money.

The tagging procedure was interesting, as we were allowed to choose the style and colour that matched our personality, encouraged by cries of 'It's so you, sir' or 'I wouldn't be seen dead in that one' which seemed like a good choice to me, given the events this morning. I discovered that a tagging bracelet was known as a 'Peckham Rolex' and was a status symbol in some parts of South London. I am sure that this would raise my street credibility with the students at the University.

I still had one last set of questions to answer before leaving the station. This was the Police 'Customer Service Questionnaire'. Recent Government policy dictated that citizens dealing with the great offices of state were to be treated as clients, and that the bureaucrats were there merely as servants of the public. Would that this be true? For example the Inland Revenue have recently been referring to me as a customer and asking 'How can we improve our service?' They could start by taking less money out of my monthly pay! I once sent back a tax demand with a note explaining that I was not interested in their scheme and could they please stop sending the circulars. In return, I received a letter demanding immediate payment or face a court order and bailiff. There was not even a 'Have a Nice Day' on the bottom of the letter.

I do not know how far this client/servant idea had spread. Had it reached the Army, I wondered. Perhaps the leaflets being dropped over remote villages in Afghanistan as shown on TV were not propaganda material, as I had assumed, but were in fact customer service questionnaires. Did the army have a Quality Standard to adhere to? They obviously had targets, hence all the shooting. What would the average Afghan villager think on receiving a typical list of questions?

HOW DID YOU HEAR ABOUT OUR PATROL?

(A tricky one this as an honest answer could lead to a fellow countryman being locked up as a spy.)

DID WE RETURN YOUR FIRE WITHIN
    a) 1 MINUTE
    b) 2 MINUTES
    c) LONGER?
HOW OFTEN DO YOU USE OUR SERVICE?
    a) ONCE IN A LIFETIME
    b) MORE, IF I CAN RUN FAST ENOUGH

And so on. I stopped this chain of thought to get on with the matter in hand, reading through the Customer Service leaflet from the police. The first questions were fairly easy.

NAME: Charles Edward Stuart
OFFENCE: Possession of an offensive cat
NAME OF ARRESTING OFFICER: ~~DI Bastard~~ DI Monro

And then it became trickier.

HOW DID YOU HEAR ABOUT US?
HOW CAN WE IMPROVE OUR SERVICE?

Still, I had help from fellow suspects. There was Frank, a serial confidence trickster whose latest wheeze was to sell Family Trees over the Internet at £50 a time. The consumer would receive a £2 packet of seed with instructions to 'Just plant the seeds, add water, and you and your family can happily watch the tree grow to its full size in less than a century.' He had earlier been implicated in a collapse of the website 'Billy No Mates Reunited.Com', losing the investors a significant amount of money. Nice chap, Frank. Then there was Ahmed, a suspected terrorist like me. He told the police that the suicide belt found in his flat was a birthday present from his mother. He told Frank and me privately that a visiting Mullah had given him the belt. The cleric had claimed that the British Army in Afghanistan were busy eradicating puppies. I thought that it was poppies, but after what happened to Lawrence I could not be so sure. The idea of meeting 70 virgins appealed to Ahmed but then, as he was from Essex, this would seem fantastical. I don't think that he was keen on the whole blowing up people bit, even to save puppies, and seemed relieved that he had been arrested.

I had trouble with:

ETHNIC ORIGIN?

And asked the Police Sergeant Dispatch Controller for his advice.

He replied in a bored fashion, reciting the answer by rote. "We strive for equal opportunity and have a policy of encouraging bio-diversity."

"I see that," I persisted, "but all of the boxes have been crossed out except this one, Chinese."

"That's right, sir, so if you would be so good to put a cross in that box, I would be much obliged. We have filled this week's quota for all the others."

It seemed pointless to argue, so I ticked Chinese as instructed and went on to the next question.

Frank thought that the idea of Sexual Orienteering was quite exciting. He had visions of running round hillsides, quite naked, his modesty covered only by a compass and a map, and wrote 'Yes please' alongside this one.

Between us, we managed to find answers to all the questions and were handed over to our respective delivery drivers. My journey was rather pleasant as Bert, my driver, meandered around the Surrey Hills, making occasionally deliveries at houses tucked away in the woods. I would be quite sorry to reach home. The final delivery was just a few streets away from my house.

There is something about another person's groceries that compels others to take a look. I had noticed this phenomenon in my local supermarket, where shoppers scanned each other's purchases with knowing, and sometimes pitying, looks. It was as if by examining the contents of a shopping basket you could look into the troubled soul of the person next to you at the checkouts. There was now a TV reality show where an up-and-coming young psychiatrist gives counselling and advice by examining of a trolley full of merchandise. His catch phrase being 'Oh dear, what have we here!' This phrase to be shouted by the studio audience as each new victim appeared on stage with his or her trolley. As I walked up the drive, I had a quick peek into the cardboard box but there was not much in there, a bottle of baby oil, sausages, cycle clips, aluminium foil and a melon amongst other things. There was nothing of real interest. I had to ring the bell twice before the door was opened. I recognised the man in the dressing gown instantly – it was Briefcase.

"I thought that you were seeing the Bishop of Guildford?"

"And I told you that I would see you tomorrow. I don't bring work home."

I also recognised the second voice floating down the stairwell. "What are you doing at the door? Are you going to take my particulars down or not?"

Not bringing work home indeed! It sounded very much to me like PC Jane. Briefcase coughed with embarrassment, snatched the groceries and with a curt "See you in the morning," he was gone.

I repeated the "See you in the morning," a few minutes later to Bert the driver as he dropped me off outside my own house, and prepared myself for the prospect that faced me within. There was not the usual struggle with the front door – it opened extremely smoothly. I made my way through to the kitchen and looked out onto the back patio.

I could see a pathetic chalked outline of Lawrence etched out on the patio. I understood why the police might want to establish the exact circumstances of Lawrence's last moments, but why was there a little chalk outline of the mouse that Lawrence had been carrying when shot. Was the mouse now stretched out on a mortuary trolley with the pathologist saying, "First impression is that you're looking for a killer with very sharp teeth, but you'll have my full report in the morning."

It was a strange experience, knowing that your every move was being watched and monitored. I could not leave the house, as any attempt to do so would undoubtedly attract the attention of Sergeant Constable and PC Sargent who I had noticed sitting in the unmarked police car parked down the road. I had no desire to be the rabbit for the police bloodhounds; besides why would I want to run away? After all, I was an innocent citizen. What did I have to fear?

The house had clearly been taken apart by the SOCO forensic team and carefully put back together again. The cupboards that had never closed properly, despite constant efforts with a screwdriver, now worked perfectly. The squeaky kitchen door had been silenced. They had also given the place a thorough dusting. An excellent job all round and I would recommend them to any DIY challenged householder, but I doubt if their number would be in *Yellow Pages*.

I tried to make sense of the day. Why did the police think that I was mixed up with terrorists? Which terrorists? How were the two Scotsmen involved? How long would I be subject to electronic surveillance? Why was I talking to myself? Ah yes, I used to talk to Lawrence. He was a very attentive listener, rarely interrupted me, and very patient until inevitably, boredom would drive him out through the cat flap to see what was happening in the real world.

The doorbell rang interrupting my thoughts. Doorbell? I was confused. I could not remember the last time the doorbell had worked. This was probably one of the reasons I did not receive many visitors. It rang again to confirm that the little treasures of SOCO had indeed restored it to operational effectiveness. By now convinced, I opened the

44

door to be faced by a small cheery man in blue overalls carrying a toolbox.

"Can I help you?" I enquired warily. Opening the front door had not been a pleasurable experience recently.

"Can I come in, I need to do some repair work."

"That's very kind of you, but I am not sure that there is anything that still needs repairing."

"Valence the name – surveillance the game. It's your tag you see. It is not working."

"When did it stop?"

"It was fine on my monitoring screen at the police station but then you disappeared somewhere in the hills south of Dorking." I followed him into the living room as he checked some kind of signal receiver.

"No… no… oh dear," he continued. "You see it's these Slovakian models. We tell them they're no good but they're cheap. Do you remember Jim Trilby, the spy who escaped to Russia? He was one of mine. And the mad mullah who escaped through Heathrow wearing a burkha; he was one of mine as well. To date I have lost, let me see, 13… no…14 suspects."

"Have you stopped anyone from fleeing?"

"Well there's you," he chuckled. "Heaven knows why you did not leg it while you had the chance. Is it all right if I open the window slightly? It sometimes helps. Clouds and other atmospherics can also be a problem."

"I don't think…" I was about to point out that the window was stiff and difficult to open but I should have known better. It slid open perfectly – SOCO again.

"Oh yes." He pushed me towards the window. "I think

that we have got something, there is a better signal here. "Could you move a little nearer… hold your left arm up… good… put your right leg on the windowsill… that's good, now hold that position."

I felt like a supermodel on a photo shoot. Perhaps I should do 'the tiger' with outstretched fingers or ruffle my fingers slowly through my hair, flashing him a sideways enigmatic pout as I did so. Better not, he might get the wrong idea.

"Perfect, now if you could stay like that while I phone the office. Oh dear." Valence looked at his mobile phone in dismay. "There's no reception. We switched to S Mobile last week to save money. The Slovakian Telephone Company claimed that there would be at least a 25% saving, which is true – a quarter of my telephone calls do not get through. Perhaps if you could stand like that while I go back to the office…"

"You are not seriously expecting me to stand here with one leg half out of the window and my left arm in the air just because the Home Office is saving money."

"Well it keeps your taxes down," said Valence helpfully. "I will be back later, unless you've done a runner," he chuckled and with that he was gone. Well, almost. It took him 10 minutes to start his car, which, I was not surprised to note, was of Slovakian manufacture.

I suddenly felt very hungry. I had not eaten anything for nearly 12 hours.

I ventured into the kitchen, which had been fully stocked when I had left home this morning. Alas, the fridge was bare. Everything presumably bagged up, numbered and taken away by forensics as potential terrorist material. I have no idea what they expected to find. I was fully aware of the explosive qualities of the American Hot Pizza that I was saving for the weekend, but how much damage could you do with a pickled gherkin?

There was that sound again, the doorbell. This time a pizza delivery courier greeted me, clad completely in white leathers topped with a white helmet. Had Munro gone soft and returned my American Hot Pizza by special delivery? On closer inspection the boxes were labelled 'The Highland Pizza Company', one of which contained as the main course a Haggis & Mozzarella flavoured pizza, and the other a side order of Gaelic Bread.

"We bean washed, so naked luke national," said a muffled voice from behind the visor.

I looked mystified, which prompted the visor to be raised and the sentence repeated.

"We're being watched, so make it look natural."

I could not see the hair, which was tucked into the helmet, but I recognised the sparkling green eyes immediately.

"Take the pizza in and I'll meet you by the back gate. Don't worry about the tag, they rarely work."

I looked at the car down the road to see what the two Special Branch men were making of this encounter. Constable was carefully checking the inside of his eyelids to ensure that no light was creeping in, while Sargent was obviously checking his share portfolio in the financial pages of the *Daily Mail* which rested on his face, the corner lifting slightly every few seconds. I had little to worry about on that front and decided that I would do as asked. Very soon I was on the back of a white Yamaha motorbike navigating the streets of Dorking at speed. I held on tight as we roared through Dorking and out onto the Guildford road. I held on tight at traffic lights, through villages and even when we had stopped and the engine was turned off. I was enjoying holding on tight, even through several millimetres of white leather. The leather made the thoughts even more interesting.

"You can let go now," came the sing-song voice.

I reluctantly obliged. We were in a lay-by that I recognised from my daily trip to work. What was new was a large bus with the inscription 'The Jacobite Conspiracy' painted in glaring colours on the side. If they were indeed Scottish Terrorists, as Munro and Cumberland had claimed, then they were certainly making no secret of it. A red-bearded, black-leather-jacketed man made his way towards us, a tartan bandana keeping the long hair out of his eyes. I assumed, and very much hoped, that Flora was not introducing me to her friends from the local Hell's Angels Chapter.

"You made it then, Flora. Hi. I'm Flora's brother, Douglas. I'll stow the bike in the luggage compartment and then we had better be off."

There was little family resemblance between brother and sister. He was stocky and of medium height and his voice was not sing-song; it growled a story. Flora was thinner and smaller, but the striking red hair was a common feature.

As he spoke, an even hairier Goth-like figure approached looking even more threatening than Douglas. His appearance would be suitable for the Headbanger at a

Conference of Headbangers. He walked towards me with his hand outstretched, which I hoped was for a handshake, and not for arm-wrestling purposes.

"Delighted to meet you. Saville-Row, James Saville-Row," he said with an impeccable cut-glass English accent. "Didn't we meet at an Eton Old Boys' Reunion?"

"I think that most unlikely," I replied.

"Must have been Cambridge then," he stated with complete assurance that this must be the case. I decided not to mention Dorking Boys' School and Brighton University.

"Let me introduce you to the rest of band," growled Douglas. "Come on board the tour bus, James will stow away the bike."

"Absolutely," confirmed James. "Anything to be of assistance. Any friend of Flora's is a friend of mine."

'The Jacobite Conspiracy' was in fact a heavy metal rock band currently making its way back to Scotland after a tour of England. I was introduced to Hamish the base player, who was to do most of the driving and Hal the drummer.

It was not long before I started dozing off and was soon dropping in and out of sleep. Subconsciously I heard bits of conversation in the background, Hamish and Hal deep in conversation about their favourite football team, which at times was incomprehensible. I gleaned that the previous manager was a turnip, but that things were looking up because their new manager was a Swede. James and Douglas were talking about creating some notoriety on stage by biting the heads off dead chickens as part of the act. James would agree to bite the heads off jelly babies but that was as far as he was prepared to go. Later, I thought I heard Flora saying "He seems a bit naïve and probably a bit of a wimp, but Uncle thinks that he might be useful and he seems nice enough."

What had possessed me to accept a lift to Scotland, where I had no plans to go, with people I hardly knew? I was too tired to care.

THURSDAY MORNING –

FLORA & FAUNA

DC Monro was feeling very pleased with himself. Thanks to some smart detective work, reports from uniform of a suspicious-looking bus just outside Dorking, and a clever deduction that 'The Jacobite Conspiracy' might have a connection with Scottish terrorism, he had arrived with his team at a narrow bridge on a lonely road south of Inverness. This time he had a proper police car, with flashing lights and everything. They had been able to outpace the slow-moving coach and set up a roadblock with the help of the local police. Charles Stuart was clearly a dangerous man, who would stop at nothing to attain his narrow political goals. Monro was leaving nothing to chance.

Cumberland was fast asleep in the back of a Volvo and, with luck, the DCI would sleep through the whole thing, leaving Monro to take all the credit.

***

Hamish, who was at the wheel, slowed the bus down to a stop. "We're at Findhorn Bridge on the High Moor but it's barricaded by the police," he declared.

After confirming this for himself, Douglas suggested that Flora and I should be prepared to make a quick exit via the back door while the band distracted the attention of the police. As he was speaking two of the policemen entered from the front of the bus.

"We're looking for a Charles Stuart," announced the first policeman brusquely, looking from side to side down the bus as he did so.

"I am Charles Stuart," declared Hamish defiantly.

"And I'm Charles Stuart," added Douglas, joining in.

"If you're looking for Charles Stuart, then look no further – for I am he," declaimed James in his best in his best Noel Coward manner.

Not to be left out Hal threw his hat into the ring. "I'm Charles Stuart, do you want to make something of it pal?"

It was vaguely reminiscent of a Stanley Kubrick film I had once seen. Hal looked threatening as he squared up to the policeman."Pick a windee," he suggested, which I gathered was Scottish for defenestration. Now we were in *Clockwork Orange* territory – real horrorshaw. Surely he was not going to pitch a policeman out of a bus window. *You can't do that Hal*, I thought – now even I was doing it! Kubrick references galore. Hal did, he threw the copper through the open window!

As the scuffle broke out at the front of the bus, Douglas had managed to open the rear door, retrieving the motorbike from the luggage compartment undetected. I was still putting my helmet on as Flora revved the engine noisily but this, unfortunately, drew attention to our mode of escape. Within a few seconds I was trying to remove my trouser leg from the vice like grip of a 2-stone police dog, when a challenging voice rang out.

"This is the police. You there, put the dog down and back off with your hands on your head."

I pointed at my chest, playing for time, and mouthed silently, 'Do you mean me?' The dog removed its teeth from my lower garment and nodded in affirmation. "Are you sure?" I asked. The dog nodded again, this time bearing its teeth. By this time Sergeant Constable had managed to grab Flora's arm and was attempting to drag her off the machine.

With a polite "Would you mind holding this?" I drove the motorbike helmet forcibly into Constable's midriff, temporarily winding him and forcing him to lose his grip on Flora.

"Come on," shouted Flora

Needing no more encouragement I mounted the pillion as Flora manoeuvred the bike round to the back of the bus, only to be confronted by DC Monro and PC Sargent. The two policemen prepared to block our way past, and were soon joined by PC Hawkins who had seen what was going on.

"Not so fast," declared Monro. Flora, taking this as a personal challenge, promptly accelerated, scattering the human barricade with ease.

We were soon off into the hills, Steve McQueen-style, and I was again clinging on tightly to Flora's waist, this time as a matter of survival rather than pleasure. Flora expertly handled the bike as she made her way up onto the High

Moor, stopping after about 5 minutes to see what was happening behind us. I could see that a Land Rover had started off in pursuit, but was now having great difficulty in crossing the burn that Flora had navigated like an Alton Towers water splash, soaking the both of us in the process. Another Land Rover was chasing several members of the Jacobite Conspiracy across the moor on the other side of the valley. I thought also that I could detect Monro and Cumberland in agitated conversation by the side of the bus. Cumberland eventually strode off with Monro offering a two-fingered salute behind his back.

We were soon on the High Moor. I had never been in such a desolate place, that is if you ignore Leatherhead on a Sunday evening. The weather pattern here could change completely within half an hour, and sure enough, although we had left the bus in bright sunshine, the sky was becoming overcast; a light drizzle soaked into any patch of clothing left dry by the earlier water jump. We made our way through the heather much to the alarm of deer, hares and other fauna who ran for their lives at this sudden noisy incursion into their daily lives. I couldn't help thinking that, as it was Thursday, I should be taking lectures on the Tudor wool trade, perhaps I should have phoned in sick. Sheep were still on the day's agenda however, as we came across a particular group of sheep that steadfastly refused to move; they were obviously made of sterner stuff than Sargent and Monro. After revving up the engine a few times, Flora ordered me to deal with the problem. And so I dismounted and approached the group who steadfastly held their ground, chewing silently. I have always found sheep difficult to deal with, mainly because they have no eyebrows and so you don't really know what they are thinking or whether they are even taking on board what you are saying. Flora became impatient during these tricky negotiations, which she demonstrated by revving the engine more frequently and shouting, "It's only a bunch of sheep, use your helmet on them; it worked earlier." Gradually I got the upper hand, as the concept of becoming a lamb chop sank in, and after a brief peer group discussion the animals turned about, ambling up the hillside muttering about off-roadsters, and we were finally able to continue on our way.

We could hear the sound of a helicopter buzzing to and fro overhead, presumably the police out of Inverness. The combination of low cloud and Flora's knowledge of places to hide prevented us from being discovered, but slowed down the journey considerably. Flora seemed to be very clear where she was headed and after nearly two hours we arrived at a building of great antiquity hidden in a fold in the moor.

The building was vacant at the moment but despite its age it was clearly lived in from time to time. It was not locked, and we were soon inside, Flora hiding the bike in an outhouse as a precaution.

"It's an old bothy owned by our family. It was derelict for years but my cousin, Brendan, recently renovated it. He's an ornithologist, an expert in Scottish birds; a Professor or something at Aberdeen University. We had better get out of these wet things," advised Flora, stripping down to her underwear in a matter of seconds. She caught my look and smiled, "You're beginning to steam up, Charles. I'll get a dressing gown." She returned with two from Brendan's bedroom. I was trying to be more discreet about my disrobement much to Flora's amusement. "You poor wee thing, trapped in a bothy with a woman of the opposite sex. And there's no phone here, you know," she said impishly. "I'll make some coffee while you finish." She busied herself with the coffee and at the same time put our wet clothes on a chair in front of the now warming Calor gas oven.

"Thank you for tackling that policeman, Charles."

"It seemed to be the right thing to do at the time, but I am not sure what I am doing here."

"I imagine that you are here because I asked you."

"Yes," I confessed. I had literally followed her to the back of beyond; a woman I hardly knew. I was on the run somewhere in Scotland chased by a motley collection of Sergeants and Constables.

"The police had told me that your name was Margaret."

"Yes, it is really. But everyone called me Marge, so I thought that if I was going to be called after a vegetable oil, I would go upmarket and call myself Flora."

I suppose this made sense in a strange kind of way.

"I am sorry that you are caught up in all this. I did try to send you a message, though."

"Ah, so you are Scheherazade."

"Yes, I am. We found out about the dawn raid, but it was a day earlier than we thought it would be."

"And what do you mean by 'all this'? Are you a Scottish Terrorist?"

Flora laughed, that engaging laugh, which with the sing-song voice was leading me ever deeper into trouble; like a siren luring me onto the rocks.

"Well I am Scottish, and my mother called me a little terror from the age of 8. So yes, I suppose I am a Scottish terrorist."

"You know what I mean, I think that I am entitled to some kind of an an explanation," I replied.

Ever since I had bumped into Flora I had been acting out the plot of John Buchan's *Thirty-nine Steps* but with additional material by Groucho Marx and Mack Sennett. If I remembered the Buchan novel correctly, within a chapter or two I would arrive at an old stately home, to be welcomed by a mysterious laird who was intent on overthrowing the state.

"You are entitled to an explanation, but you will have to wait until we reach my uncle's place. We are not far, and hopefully the police will not look for us there. I am sure that if they did find us, you would soon sort them out. You were very brave back there," said Flora turning in my direction.

I blushed; I had myself been quite surprised by my audacity. "Do you mean at the bridge?"

"No, with the sheep. At one point they had you surrounded and I thought that your number was up. But you stared them all out, especially the mean-looking one at the front with the cauliflower ear."

She was teasing me again, laughing all the while, but I could not bring myself to be offended, not by Flora.

Our eyes met. I was not sure whether it was the coffee, or the proximity of Flora, but I was feeling a little flushed. I was beginning to feel quite passionate about the woman that, until last night, I knew virtually nothing about. And now here we were, sitting in a remote spot with only dressing gowns between us. What was a man to do?

At this point there was intended to be the obligatory sex scene demanded by the publishers to sell more books. The publishers work on the basis that, in any thriller, the readers remember who did what to whom, and how, rather than 'who dun it'. Unfortunately the author was unable to complete this section due to his lack of experience and imagination. We have therefore included the author's notes for this scene, and a blank sheet of paper, so that those readers with suitable experience can complete the scene for themselves.

IDEAS FOR SEX SCENE CHAPTER 5

Hard Nipples

Tattoo on left breast

Melon

Yes! Yes! Yes!

Bicycle clips

Creamy White Skin

Johnston's Baby Oil

Firm young buttocks

A4 Batteries

Kama Sutra

Nubile Young Flesh

Ripe Tomatoes

Lost in the moment of Passion

Delicately Curved Neck

Small Shapely Breasts

Aluminium Foil

Fly Swatter
Passion Fruit
Erotic Sweaty Odour
Underarm Deodorant
Bicycle Pump
Sausages

Note

It is believed that the Author was preparing a shopping list at the same time as compiling these notes. After a fierce debate, the editorial team were unable to reach a consensus on which items were clearly not needed for mad passionate sex, and which must have been part of the shopping list. We have therefore included the list in its entirety, to enable readers to make up their own minds. We take no responsibility for any subsequent injuries that may result.

This space is reserved for the Reader to complete the sex scene. Alert readers will note that some of the items listed above appeared in the shopping basket of 'Briefcase'. If you need help with this page, the office number of Briefcase, Sue and Billem is Dorking 985614.

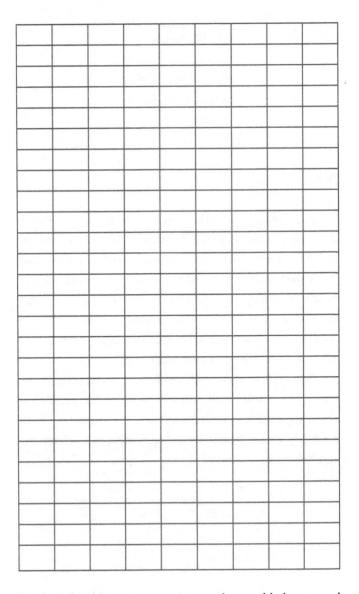

Readers should now stop writing, take a cold shower and move in an orderly fashion to the next page.

I was woken up by the sound of a vehicle on the gravel outside, the reflection of the lights bouncing around in the dusk. I had obviously been fast asleep for some hours as the light was fading outside. Flora was fully dressed while I was still in my underwear covered by a flimsy dressing gown.

"Ah. You're awake. Your clothes are dry, but your trousers were ruined when you were playing with that dog. I've got you out a pair of Brendan's, I am sure he won't mind. Anyway we can ask him, that's his Land Rover pulling up. By the way, Brendan can get a bit passionate about the feathered fraternity so don't say anything too provocative."

"Like what? How can I offend a professional twitcher?"

"Using expressions like 'Stone the Crows' or 'Dead Duck'. Recently one of his students suffered a spoonerism by saying 'leaving no turn un-stoned'. Brendan was bound over to keep the peace for three months after that little incident."

"I shall be very careful. I won't act like a complete tit."

"Charles…!"

"Only joking."

Brendan entered the room. He had the family trademark red beard, the men that is, with that ruddy complexion that comes from too long spent out in the open air. His head moved from side to side in conjunction with his eyes in a strange jerky movement. Watching too many birds, I supposed.

"I thought it must be you," said Brendan spotting Flora.

"I hope that you don't mind."

"Of course not."

"And this is Charles Stuart."

Brendan jerked his head in my direction. I could see the look of disappointment in his face.

Flora had also detected the change in mood. Presumably she was worried that Brendan might take instant flight and hurriedly added, "Not the real Charles Stuart, but I can vouch for him none the less."

I nodded in confirmation and Brendan seemed to relax.

"Are you hungry? Have you had anything to eat?" he enquired.

"Yes, we found some sausages and tomatoes, and there was some melon and passion fruit in the cooler," replied Flora.

(Some readers should now be ashamed of themselves. The Editor.)

"And I have borrowed a pair of your trousers for Charles, if you don't mind."

"Not at all. What else can I do for you?"

"It would be very kind if you could take us to Uncle's at Castle Brady."

"We'll leave first thing in the morning," said Brendan.

"We would like to go as soon as possible, you see we are on the run from the police."

"That explains a lot. Findhorn Village Police Station was like a First World War casualty clearing station this afternoon. Some men with splints, others with slings. You haven't been roughing up policemen again have you, little cousin?"

"Certainly not, I had Dougal and the band to do that for me and, of course, Charles here."

I blanched at the thought of roughing up policemen. Not something that I previously had a reputation for.

Brendan tapped a few times on a barometer attached to the wall just inside the door. The barometer is an instrument designed to tell you what the weather is like outside. Invented in the 17th century, it gradually replaced the window, which had previously been used for this purpose. This is presumably why Georgian houses have so many bricked-up redundant windows. I could easily see for myself, through the side window, that the drizzle had stopped and that the low cloud had cleared.

"Looks as though it is clearing up outside. We'll be able to leave right away," confirmed Brendan, "but I should warn you that the area is crawling with police. Not just the usual ones from Nairn and Inverness, but some very strange types from London. Sergeant Fraser is tearing his hair out at the mess they are making of his police station."

THURSDAY EVENING –

A PIG WITH LIPSTICK ON STILL LOOKS LIKE A PIG

Professor Duncan Renfrew should have been a household name, a name on everyone's lips. A name that would have symbolised the great leap in scientific understanding that took place during the mid-nineteenth century. An undistinguished Victorian Professor of Natural History at Edinburgh University, Renfrew had taken to holidaying on the shores of Moray Firth with his faithful dog, Albert. It was during these walks that the Professor made an observation that he thought was 'most singular'. The inhabitants of the coastline nearest to The Highlands were all short and stocky. His subsequent research showed that the stature of the population changed noticeably the nearer you were to Lossiemouth, the more easterly population being taller and thinner. He mentioned this to his good friend Charles Darwin, the soon-to-become famous naturalist, and suggested that this could be something to do with the strong westerly winds that the Firth experienced. Asked to elaborate, Renfrew explained his view that the human population had somehow adapted over the years to the conditions. Being short and stocky was appropriate for the Findhorn area to minimise the chances of being blown over, but with the wind level dropping as you ventured further east, this requirement became unnecessary. 'Of course,' agreed Darwin, 'the wind,' suddenly realising the principle that had been eluding him all those years since he had recorded his findings on the finches of the Galapagos Islands. With this sudden insight, he was quickly able to complete and present his controversial paper 'On the Origin of Species by Means of Natural Selection' to the Linnean Society, and the rest, as they say, is history. Professor Renfrew's paper 'On the Origin of Short Stocky People in The Findhorn Area' was politely received by the Society, but soon forgotten.

Had the Professor been around 150 years later, he would have found a perfect example for his research in Sergeant Duncan Fraser, the man in charge of the Findhorn Police Station. Shaped like a milk churn, and with a very low centre of gravity, it would take a force 9 gale to knock him over. With the growth of travel, and general mixing of populations, the people of Findhorn no longer resembled a set of skittles, but Fraser would definitely have qualified to be pinned inside a specimen cabinet in Renfrew's study. His other physical attributes included a midge-spearing moustache, oversize ears that made him resemble a Greek amphorae, and a weather-beaten face displaying constant surprise that anything could possibly happen that involved him in any way, particularly where this might involve some work on his part.

To say that Fraser disliked crime was an understatement. In fact he hated it with a passion. Crime required crime reports, and Fraser had not joined the police force to fill in forms. Forms filled him with dread and could quickly induce a form of paralysis, with the Sergeant sitting at his desk bathed in a cold sweat, for hours at a time. He had wanted to follow in his father's footsteps, becoming a respected member of the local community without having to sully his hands with work. There were few problems that could not be sorted out by a sharp word or a clip round the ear. As a result, the only recorded crime locally in the last few years was the vandalised speed camera on the B9011. Three times it had been replaced and three times it had been set on fire. Fraser had of course made some desultory house-to-house enquires without really expecting anyone to name the person responsible. But then, as he was the culprit, this did not really matter. 'The Infernal One-Eyed Monster', as Fraser called it, created piles of paperwork and clearly had to go. Fraser did not want to suffer from piles.

From time to time there were questions asked at Nairn Police Headquarters about the lack of crime in the Findhorn area. One school of thought said this showed the excellent work put in by Sergeant Fraser, an idea actively encouraged by the Sergeant himself. The more serious police hierarchy were not so sure, and from time to time a senior officer was sent out to see what was going on. Fraser had a well-worked coping strategy for this.

Each such visit seemed to coincide with a serious case of rare bird egg theft that Fraser had been working on for some time. Full of enthusiasm the visiting officer would be taken up onto the High Moors for an avian stake-out, which was generally located in the most un-hospitable place imaginable. Lighting a fire would be out of the question as it would reveal the police presence and usually, after several uncomfortable days and nights living off sandwiches and cold tea, the senior officer would throw in the towel and report back to HQ on Fraser's single-mindedness and dedication to duty.

Eventually the Assistant Chief Constable decided to look for himself. He survived a week before being airlifted to Inverness with pneumonia and frostbite. Strangely Fraser himself did not seem to suffer on these outings in quite the same way. Despite the fact that, no matter how filthy the weather, he would insist on going out on patrol to see if he could flush out the miscreants. The visiting officer would dutifully train the binoculars and camera on a particular rock face as instructed, while Fraser would disappear off into the sleet in an out-flanking movement. This patrol would usually end at Brendan MacDonald's bothy, where the Sergeant would be warmly greeted with a hot toddy and a bowl of broth. Fraser would always be disappointed on returning to the stake-out to find that the visiting officer had not managed to catch on film the egg thieves that the Sergeant was certain that he had flushed out.

There had been no more interlopers at Fraser's police station after the Assistant Chief Constable; that is until that evening when the Special Branch officers turned up from London. He couldn't abide Senior Officers at the best of times, and now he was saddled with Cumberland and Monro who were two of the most obnoxious Police Officers he had come across; and both were Sassenachs as well. They had five of their own men backed up with a detachment from the Inverness force. The tiny Findhorn Station was very overcrowded. Additional communication equipment was being installed, incident boards set up, and additional tables and chairs squeezed in wherever possible. There had not been such activity in the station since… Well to be frank, activity of any kind was most unusual.

Monro started the conversation off, "Sergeant Fraser, you probably wonder why we are here."

"Not at all. You are either here on police business or you are here for the Findhorn International Ceilidh and Dog Show, and I don't see any dogs."

"Both, in fact the two are related," replied Monro, ignoring the mild sarcasm. "Have you heard of a man called Charles Stuart?"

"The Prince over the Water?"

"Yes. We believe that he is now over here and in this area. We nearly caught him this morning a few miles from here, but he escaped with an accomplice. Our information is that he is now in the Findhorn Village area. We also believe that he is here to meet with a gang of terrorists who are planning a bid to overthrow the government and monarchy, and then declaring this man to be a king."

"And this is considered to be a bad thing, I suppose," responded the Sergeant pushing his insubordination a bit too far.

"Of course it is. I expect you to do your duty Fraser; if not I will soon find someone else to do your job."

"I will do my duty to my country, sir. Have no fears on that score."

Cumberland appeared to be satisfied with this ambiguous reply. "Have you noticed any unusual activity around here recently?" he enquired.

"You mean apart from my Police Station being swamped by Special Branch Officers from England? Well last week I did notice some strange activity on the High Moor. Could be terrorists in training. I will take you there for a covert surveillance operation if you like," suggested Fraser falling back on his tried and tested routine.

"We don't have time for that. Besides, we believe that the meeting will take place at a show, the Findhorn Ceilidh and Dog Show."

"International Ceilidh and Dog Show," corrected Fraser.

"Whatever," answered Cumberland irritably, without looking up. It seemed to Fraser that the DCI was busy doodling in his notebook. "We will need to go undercover for an operation like this. We will need to blend in and observe."

"Blend in and observe," confirmed Monro.

"And how do you propose to do that?" asked the Sergeant.

"I think that we will need some dogs for the dog show," said Monro, thinking out loud.

"But I don't have any dogs! And most dog owners will be taking theirs to the show."

"Then you'll have to find some," insisted Monro.

"I'll try, but I can't promise anything," muttered Fraser.

"And we'll need some sort of disguise for the ceilidh," continued Monro.

"That will be easier. There are a lot of acts playing that night." Fraser reached over on his desk and grabbed the weighty programme for the show.

"Can you play the pipes?"

"No."

"The mouth organ?"

"The fiddle… the piano… the celeste… the crumhorn…"

"No."

"Ah, how about this one. 'The Findhorn Swingers'."

"Are they what I think they are?" asked Monro suspiciously.

"A 40s dance band, led by Madge Baker, they're very keen. They are always in and out of each other's houses practising, especially 'In the Mood'."

"In the mood for what!" asked Monro becoming more alarmed.

"Sometimes there are small groups trying out something new – you can tell by the groans which can be heard all over the village. And occasionally the whole ensemble will get together in the hall. We usually have the St John's Ambulance standing by in case someone is injured. Madge is a hard taskmaster and can get quite excited when whipping the band into shape."

It did not sound promising. "Anything else?" asked Cumberland.

"Ah, here's one. 'The Norse Dancers' are putting on a display."

"Is that the one where you ponce around in a funny hat, cymbals on your ankles, and at the same time waving a couple of white handkerchiefs over your head, pretending to be a country yokel? Or worse, leaping up and down pretending to hit each other with sticks," sneered Monro.

"Similar, but that would be Morris Dancers, the English version," explained the Sergeant, "which originates from the effete Sassenach culture. Ours is more interesting and is derived from the Viking Norse culture. Mind you since Health and Safety got involved it is not quite as violent as it used to be. Only 4 people went to hospital last year."

Cumberland and Monro looked at each. Monro spoke for them both.

"And the chance of survival if our identity is suspected?"

"Ah. I see your point, perhaps that isn't suitable."

"Scottish Country Dancing, 'Maclaren's Reel' and all that?"

"I'm afraid not," replied Cumberland. Monro nodded in confirmation.

"Have you got a thong?"

"NO," exclaimed Monro and Cumberland in unison.

"Can you blow ping pong balls out of your bottom?"

"Surely there isn't anyone doing that?"

"No, but I thought I would ask. I've heard about it but I've never seen it done."

"I've got it. There is a fancy dress competition, to be judged during the ceilidh. I could ring round for some costumes."

"Well if that's all there is, then we have no choice," decided Cumberland. "Please find us costumes that are sensible and in keeping with our status as policemen. No bags marked swag, or Mafia outfits."

"It won't be easy, but I should be able to find something." There was a local saying, thought Fraser; a pig with lipstick on is still a pig. How on earth was he to disguise a pasty-faced beanpole, and his rotund, red-faced sidekick.

DC Monro wasn't happy, he had a bad feeling about this but had to go along with his superior's decision.

Cumberland changed the subject. "Do you have any maps of Findhorn, I intend to carry out house-to-house interviews tomorrow morning."

Fraser was appalled. "I am not sure that is such a good idea, sir. They don't like strangers knocking on doors here. We once had a canvasser for the Liberal Democrats. He managed three houses before he was airlifted to Inverness General Hospital."

"We're Special Branch, we won't stand any nonsense. My men can look after themselves."

Fraser looked through the door at a number of policemen, some with bandages, others limping and one man with a crutch. The Sergeant had heard about the Battle of Findhorn Bridge with the members of 'The Jacobite Conspiracy'. Come to think of it, the DCI and Monro also looked slightly the worse for wear. *But it's their funeral,* he thought. Monro summoned two of the other casualties into the office.

"This is Police Constable Sargent and Sergeant Constable. I want you to brief them about the village."

"Aren't those names a bit confusing, Constable?" observed Fraser.

"Why?" said Sargent and Constable in unison, looking puzzled.

Fraser reluctantly produced a map of the village and pored over it with Sargent and Constable taking copious notes. *A true professional approach*, thought Monro.

"This is the police station," advised Fraser pointing to a circled building in the middle of the map. "This is the pub, the Rebel & Gibbet, and over here is the Church of the Blessed Marilyn. Oh, and this building over here is the Spar."

The visiting police officers were impressed and smiled at each other as they had the same thought. Perhaps after the final arrests they could stay on and reinvigorate their bodies, treat the sprains and strains with a massage and a sauna at the spa. Fraser could not understand why they seemed so excited about a grocery shop.

Having described the major landmarks in Findhorn and the focal points of his daily routine, with the exception of the Church of course, he stood back with his arms folded, as if to say, "Over and Out."

"That's about it," he confirmed, "that's all I've ever needed to know."

"But what about the houses where people live?" asked Monro, irritated.

"All together more tricky," advised Fraser, "hard to tell who is who or where, most of the time. This one here is the house of Madge Baker. I think that you'll find Mr Burgess here most of the time. Except on Wednesdays and Thursdays when he visits Aberdeen, then Mr Faulkner will probably answer the door."

"And this one next door to it?" asked Constable.

"No one knows. The door hasn't been answered for years, although the lights go on and off, occasionally."

"And this one? Who will answer the door here?"

"No one, I hope. That's Jim Grundy's house. He is due to be buried in the kirk graveyard on Monday morning. He originally left his body to medical science, but Edinburgh University disputed the will and won. He then wanted to be cremated, but having consumed so much Scotch in his lifetime, the Council decided that he might be a fire hazard and ordered a burial. He was Findhorn's oldest man, or so he claimed, but we all know that he lied about his age. He claimed that he was 12 when the Kitchener men were recruiting, but it was believed hereabouts that he was then in his mid 20s."

"I don't need a life history," said Monro, irritated, "just the names and a brief description."

"Just giving you a bit of background, it might be relevant. Now let me see. This one here is Ferguson, the trombone player in the Findhorn Swingers, so he could be anywhere in the village, working on his vibrato with one of the others. Mrs Ferguson might be here or... here, fiddling with Mr Beattie. In fact, it is probably best if I mark all the houses of the Swingers and you can tell me who's where at the moment.

"You're taking the piss, aren't you?" said Monro.

"I am just telling it like it is, sir."

Cumberland seemed to be paying little attention to the conversation as he worked on his latest doodle, a tuba blowing air up the skirts of a person with a red dress, seeming to recreate the famous Marilyn Monroe film scene. Only the face of the Monro sketched was more Detective Inspector than Norma Jean.

Monro was becoming quite aggressive. "Listen Fraser, I don't want to hear any more about randy musicians, senior citizens who are fire hazards, or who is fiddling with whom, I just want names to match the addresses on this map."

"This is ridiculous," interjected Cumberland. "Constable, get a copy of the electoral roll straight away. Wake up the Mayor if you have to. We'll make a start on the house-to-house at first light."

"Yes, Gov," was the response delivered in perfect two-part harmony. No one seemed in the least surprised at this.

THURSDAY NIGHT –

MEET THE ANCESTORS

It was fully dark by the time that Brendan dropped us off at Castle Brady.

He had navigated the highways and byways with great care, frequently stopping and listening before turning off for a cross-country leg, avoiding certain junctions and crossings. On several occasions Brendan stopped and turned the engine off. The silence on these occasions was shattered by the hoot of an owl, so close that it made me jump. I was convinced that Brendan was using a form of aerial surveillance to avoid police patrols.

The towers and fake castellations made Castle Brady look sinister and forbidding by the light of the half moon. The occasional outbreaks of barking from a group of nearby dogs did nothing to dispel the idea that we had arrived in central Transylvania. Fiona hauled on a chain that was attached to the heavy oak front door and somewhere inside the house, but a long way inside, there was the muffled sound of a bell ringing, which echoed several times before fading away. After several minutes, the door was opened by a hard-looking man in black boots, jodhpurs and wearing a cruel-looking scar running from his left ear to the top of his lip.

"*Guten Abend, Fraulein*," he said with a thick Germanic accent. Looking at me he added, "The Colonel is expecting you, Herr Stuart."

We were joined by the housekeeper, a frumpish woman, grey hair held tight in a bun and with an apron so starched that there was a definite cracking noise as she leaned over to take Flora's things. " You must be worn out by your wanderings." She gave me a disapproving stare up and down, starting and finishing with Brendan's trousers. I think that she must have recognised the garment and, putting two and two together had concluded that, if I had put Brendan's on, then at some point I must have taken mine off.

"A young lady like you shouldn't be out on the High Moor with strangers. Anything could have happened."

"Nothing happened Mrs McGregor, does Charles look like the sort of man that would take advantage of me?"

I tried desperately to not look like the sort of man that would take advantage of Flora, although when Mrs McGregor continued with, "We had better get you upstairs and out of your clothes, young miss," the expression on my face betrayed my inner thoughts, confirming the housekeeper's already low opinion of me.

Erik quickly ushered me down a long corridor furnished with suits of armour, and paintings that I assumed were family portraits. All apart from the ones of pigs that is, unless of course there had been some severe inbreeding in the past.

The Colonel was waiting for us in his study, sitting in an upright leather armchair with a cigar in one hand and a glass of whisky in the other.

Colonel Angus MacPherson, formerly of the Black Watch, was a frightening-looking character. Known as 'Fearsome MacPherson' to his troops, he was 6'4" tall, built like a bull, and with one of those prickly moustaches that prove useful for spearing flies and other insects on overseas postings. He had the typical booming voice and iron handshake associated with the military.

"You will have a wee dram," he barked, his eyelids raised in an exaggerated manner making his expression slightly manic. It was clearly a statement, not a question. "Then sit yourself down."

Erik excused himself with much clicking of heels and without, I was surprised to note, the Nazi salute that I was half expecting. The Colonel read my thoughts.

"He's quite harmless. The scar was from Chelsea supporters at an England–Germany friendly in '88. The rest of the outfit he feels gives him some authenticity as Head of Security. I came across him during my British Army of the Rhine days. Strange business, whole Regiment was on parade ground at Minden for one of those aerial group photos that the Army likes. You know, the ones where all the soldiers stand in a semicircle in front of their vehicles, with the senior officers and the regimental goat standing in the middle of the hemisphere, all looking up saying 'Cheese'. Unfortunately, some men were standing there with no vehicles behind them. We were short of two Bedford lorries and one Scout car. It was all highly embarrassing. I and two other Lieutenants were told to find them and Sergeant Gordon, my orderly, suggested that I have a word with Erik. I recognised him, having seen him around the camp a few times before, but without being really sure why he was there. According to Gordon, Erik could 'fix' anything; the Regiment couldn't operate without him. After a judicious contribution from Regimental funds the missing vehicles reappeared. Well, not the ones we had lost but their exact equivalents from elsewhere. I did not want to know where from, I was just glad that they materialised. Some years later I did notice that a contemporary photo of the Gloucestershire Regiment looked like a smile with 3 teeth missing! The soldiers were all saying 'Cheese' but the officers just looked cheesed off. Erik has been helping me out of fixes ever since."

Four wee drams later, or more precisely a wee bottle later, he was well into his military reminiscences.

"Falkland Islands. Bloody good war! Faulty maps, climbed wrong bloody hill, full of Argies. Proper fight – lost half of unit. All hushed up afterwards.

"Iraq. Good fighters, the towel heads. Got caught in an ambush. Bloody good scrap. Lost half of unit. Towel heads turned out to be Yanks. Faulty recognition beacon. All hushed up of course."

"Last year went to Afghanistan. Went to eradicate puppies or some such."

So Ahmed was right, after all. The British were eradicating puppies!

"Good men, the Afghans. Give you a bloody good cup of tea, shake your hand and then shoot at you as you leave the village."

"Lost half of unit?" I asked politely.

"Lost half of unit before we got there, faulty compass apparently. Funny thing, chaps didn't turn up again until just before we were due to fly back home."

He seemed genuinely puzzled by this act of self-preservation. Clearly he was unaware that roaming bits of the globe once coloured red and engaging in 'bloody good fights' with exotic locals had gone out of fashion since he had studied Kipling at school. Given the MacPherson family battle honours, the soldiers would have been safer with the Taliban.

Rising from the armchair he wandered round the room inspecting some of his illustrious ancestors.

"Always been an Army family. Great-great grandfather was in the Crimean War. Charged wrong bloody guns, lost half of unit. Now that was a bloody good fight!"

The list was endless. It was clear that there was a continuing family resemblance – his ancestors seemed to have been present, or responsible for, every disaster befalling the British Army since 1792.

"Lost Great Uncle Jack at Christmas 1914," he said pointing to one of the family portraits.

"At Ypres, I assume?"

"Yes. Funny thing. Got into an argument with a couple of Bosch about the offside rule in football. Observer, thinking punch-up was a trench raid, sent a whole bloody barrage down. All that they found of Jack was his football, which was buried with full military honours. All hushed up of course. Jack got a posthumous medal for his part in stopping the raid.

"In fact the military were so cross that they invented a new medal, originally just for Jack. Called it the Military Cross in a rare sense of humour. Bosch thought whole thing was damned unsporting, especially as they were 3 – 1 up at the time. No more Christmas truces after that."

"What about that one?" I pointed to the picture of the fine-looking young man dressed in a uniform that seemed to me of Napoleonic vintage. "He was obviously not in the Army."

"Yes, you're right. That is Captain James MacPherson RN. Tragic story. Nelson wanted him to be shot for insubordination. He had been ordered to call out the guard and according to Nelson, who was quite mad by this time, James had replied 'Eye, eye Admiral,' and then called out 'Too arms, too arms'. Nelson said that he could not see the joke, even with his good eye! Luckily both were killed at Trafalgar, avoiding a farcical court martial. MacPhersons avoided the Navy after that, apart from George."

"What happened to George?"

"Nobody knows, or what happened to his crew."

There was a firm knock at the door. "Come," barked the Colonel.

It was Sergeant Gordon. "Begging your pardon sir. It's the Major, he's escaped again."

"And what was it this time?" MacPherson enquired.

"Erik thinks that it was a variation of 87, sir."

The Colonel explained, "It's my father. Captured at Dunkirk. Faulty radio."

"Slovakian?" I asked. The Colonel looked at me as if I was mad and continued the story.

"Didn't hear the order to retreat. Surrounded by Jerry. Put up a bloody good fight."

"Lost half of unit," said the Sergeant, the Colonel and I in unison.

"Put in prison for rest of war. Bloody good officer. Made 23 escapes in 5 years. Almost made it once. Disguised himself as a priest and got as far as Donauworth in Bavaria, heading for the Swiss border. Got carried away and agreed to carry out a wedding. Managed pretty well by sticking entirely to Latin. By all accounts, lovely wedding.

"Still gets postcards from the grandchildren. But the local wine at the reception did for him. Toasted bride and groom in English and then led a sing-song. Local policeman toasted Major's health in German and then arrested him. Went arm in arm to the police station singing 'Lily Marlene'. Still gets Christmas cards from old Kurt."

He dismissed the Sergeant, "Get Erik to put out the usual search parties, there's a good fellow."

"Surely he can't be in any harm?" I asked. "Is it his age?"

"Good Lord no! Strong as an ox and cunning as a fox. Trouble is, every time he gets out he still heads for Zurich. Thinks he is still in Stalag XXI in 1943." The Colonel went to the bookshelf and pulled out a well-thumbed volume, which he explained was the old man's wartime memoirs, *All Out War – the Man They Couldn't Keep In*.

"Ah. The old 87." The Colonel obviously thought that no further explanation was needed.

"Started in the 50s. He 'escaped' from our base in Kyrenia disguised as a Turkish belly dancer. God knows how with his knees. Spent 3 months in the Troodos

Mountains with EOKA guerrillas. He thought they were French Macquis. Provided MI5 with lots of useful information and awarded MC for undercover work. All had to be hushed up. Then there was that problem in Malaya, which has never been properly explained," he said with a puzzled frown but without elaborating.

"Sent back to staff duties at Sandhurst, considered to be a harmless job. All fine for a while, until the episode of the Royal passing out parade. It was all very embarrassing. Palace staff were adamant that all Ladies in Waiting had returned with the Queen's party. The naked woman found in the stationery cupboard could not possibly be one of theirs. Lady Fiona was very good about it and was made comfortable in one of the student's residences. In the end she was quite disappointed to leave. The gallant young officers had made sure that she did not want for anything. Every need was satisfied whatever the time of day or night.

"The Major was also having a good time until he was finally rumbled by Prince Philip, the Prince receiving quite a shock in the process.

"We tried a retired officer's home on one occasion. Lovely place, lovely matron." The Colonel was deep in thought for a moment and then recounted the story.

"All went well at first, until the 'Weapon Inspection'. Every Wednesday Matron would take one of the boys into her office for a health check. The chosen man would take off all his clothes for a full kit inspection. Of course they were all used to this from their military service. When it came to the Major's turn, he didn't disappoint. Matron was very pleased, disrobed herself and, with a wink, made her way to the sofa."

"I can see where this is heading, Zurich?"

"Yes, I'm afraid so. He grabbed her clothes, out through the patio door, and across the lawn with Matron in hot pursuit. The croquet players he passed did not recall this being listed in the day's activities, but enthusiastically stripped off to join in nevertheless. The 'privates' on display consisted of an Admiral, two Colonels and a full General. Matron rushed between them, a flapping white expanse with billowing breasts reminding the Admiral of the glory days of the Tea Clippers in full sail. A tear came to his eye as he stood with the others, fully erect, forming a rather unusual guard of honour. As the Major disappeared into the shrubbery at the bottom of the garden, Matron decided that four in the hand was worth one in the bush, although one in the bush had been her intention all along. She allowed herself to be caught just outside the summerhouse, protesting ever so slightly as she was carried inside. 'Croquet Manoeuvres' became a regular Wednesday activity after that."

"And the Major?"

"Made it to Zurich and did a stint as a Matron at a Swiss finishing school; after all, he had the uniform for it. Had a whale of a time especially at lights out. If it weren't for the steamy lesbian affair with the Headmistress he would still be there. He humoured her for a while with kisses and a little bit of controlled petting, but one night was taken completely by surprise and tied to the bedstead. The Headmistress stripped him slowly to the background music of 'Bolero' until, inevitably shocked and disappointed, she ran out screaming. He was discovered the next day by two of the young students who after satisfying their curiosity phoned the police. The Headmistress spent the rest of her days in a convent, praying for forgiveness."

"And what happened to the Major?"

"It hardly seems fair, but he was deported for indecent exposure."

The Major sounded like quite a character. I wondered if I would get to meet him.

The Colonel wandered over to the far wall, lined with the older paintings. Stopping before a particular group he took a breath to emphasise the importance of his next statement. "And these are the MacPhersons who fought in what the history books call the Jacobite Rebellions – the attempt to restore the Stuarts to their rightful throne. Taking their part in the glorious battles against the English, Dunkeld, Killiekrankie, Preston Pans and Falkirk. And, of course the most glorious of them all, Culloden, just a short way down the Firth from here. That's where, on that fateful afternoon in 1746, the pride of Scotland lost their lives." MacPherson was speaking as if the events had taken place only a few days before.

Before I had a chance to ask exactly what I had stumbled into, he seemed to have guessed my thoughts. "You are probably wondering what's going on, and why you are here."

"It had crossed my mind that there was probably a reason why I was being chased across the country by the police. They seem to think that I am involved in terrorism."

"Well, there will be time enough for the telling tomorrow, laddie. I have to be up early for a training session, and I'm sure that you must be tired after your journey so I think that it might be time to retire."

"But why am I here? Can't you at least tell me that?"

"Only you can say. After all, we didn't kidnap you."

"But there has to be some reason why I'm here," I persisted.

"And where is Flora?" asked the Colonel.

"Upstairs, I should imagine."

"Then just possibly, laddie, that is why you are here. Now I'll show you to your room and bid you good night."

He was right, of course.

Editor's Note

At this point readers may care to read Appendix 1 concerning the historical background to the Jacobite Rebellions.

FRIDAY MORNING –

BARKING MAD

I had the strangest dream. I dreamt that two men dressed as Civil War cavaliers were hitting me repeatedly over the head with a wet fish. I had no idea why, although it probably had something to do with a story about a long-dead MacPherson. This could account for my throbbing forehead, although the content of the Colonel's drinks cabinet was the more likely culprit. Whatever the reason, the result was that I had great difficulty getting out of bed. It had been light for some hours before I managed to haul myself up to a vertical position.

The last time I had felt like this was after that stag night in Estonia, when I woke up to find the new Mrs Stuart in my bed. It was a strange experience to go to a friend's stag night without realising that it is also your own. Stranger still when you discover that the only words of English your new bride can speak are 'I do', although for our entire marriage she didn't. She took up pole-vaulting instead. From that day to this I had decided to avoid excessive alcohol; I wasn't to know exactly how many MacPhersons had met their end in strange and mysterious circumstances, often in strange and mysterious countries. Each story necessitated 'a wee dram' for the telling, and it was with great difficulty that I finally made my way upstairs to bed, noting thankfully that we had saved the portraits in the corridors for another day.

I was the last down for breakfast, which did not improve Mrs McGregor's attitude. I asked whether I could have a full English breakfast, which I knew was a mistake as soon as I had said it. The look on her face was as if I had asked for a hamster on toast washed down with a glass of virgin's blood.

"There's only bannock and black pudding left," she declared icily and pointed to a side table laden with these delicacies. I assumed that 'bannock' was the oatcake occupying the space next to the black pudding.

"What else I have missed?" I said, not relishing the thought of that menu on my queasy stomach.

She frowned before responding. "It's a Friday – there is only bannock and black pudding on a Friday."

"Bannock and black pudding it is then," I replied cheerily trying to get on her good side, and sat down with a plate of rock-hard oatcake and cold black pudding. Mrs McGregor ostentatiously cleared up the breakfast plates and generally tidied everything away very noisily for my benefit. I had kept her waiting after all.

"Mrs McGregor, could I possibly have the pepper?" I enquired.

This provoked another frown, following which Mrs

McGregor left the room briefly and returned with a copy of *The Findhorn News*.

"You'll not be sitting here all morning reading the paper, I trust."

This not intended to be a question. However, seeing that the leading story was about the opening of the new Culloden visitor centre that week, I did spend rather a long time, and this did nothing to improve my relationship with Mrs McGregor, or my relationship with the black pudding, which was slowly congealing. The Queen was to perform the opening ceremony at the new centre on Sunday, the 260th Anniversary of the Battle, accompanied by the Prime Minister. Culloden! If MacPherson was typical of the native population, you would have thought that Her Majesty would have found an excuse to visit Amritsar, Ommdurman, or the Khyber Pass, where local memories of the British Army had perhaps faded by now; not Culloden.

I chased the pepperless black pudding around the plate a few times under the disapproving eye of Mrs McGregor who had that 'you cannot leave the table until you have eaten it all' look. Finally, I was able to effect an escape during her brief absence from the dining room on a plate-banging, point-making exercise. Pocketing the oatcakes and black pudding so as not to cause further offence by leaving them behind, I managed to make it out of the front door without being spotted.

Temporarily blinded by the bright sunshine, I followed the sound of Sergeant Gordon's shouts to the training ground, intrigued to see what the Colonel would be like in his professional environment.

I had often seen films of terrorists training on the news. Scenes of men laughing and smiling at the camera, brandishing wooden guns as they crawled through pretend minefields. Or grim-faced men with raised fists and Kalashnikovs, chanting slogans about the imminent demise of their government, imperialist capitalism, the West in general or all three.

It was not at all what I had expected. There was the Colonel, looking every inch the officer – dressed in combat fatigues with swagger stick in hand, and a tam-o'-shanter perched precariously on his grey hair. He looked on approvingly as four men, similarly dressed in combat fatigues, walked round a marked-out arena, each with a Scottie dog on the end of a lead. I stood open-mouthed as Sergeant Gordon put the handlers and dogs through a rapid routine of wheels, turns and diagonal criss-crossing of the arena. As precision drills went it was certainly impressive, if perhaps militarily doubtful.

"Assault course… wait for it… go," barked the Sergeant and was immediately answered by the noise of the excited Scotties climbing over obstacles, disappearing down plastic tunnels and reappearing, tails wagging, at the other end. What on earth was going on? What on earth did he hope to achieve with an army of Scottie dogs?

"Are there more units of Scottie dogs in training?" I enquired.

"Aye, there are. Also Spaniels, Collies and other breeds," replied the Colonel.

I was incredulous. "May I ask why?"

"Deception, laddie, an important military stratagem.

We need a way of travelling around the country to meet up with our lads and lassies without arousing police suspicion. We tried other methods without success."

"Such as?"

"Orienteering. Met up at events. Lost many brave men that way. And then there was… ah… yes, there was a period when we tried ballroom dancing competitions. Not enough women recruits so some of the lads had to dress up in frocks, tutus etc. Funny business though, some of them quite liked it. The Major helped the keen ones by advising on gowns, nylons, sequin sewing, that sort of thing. We only found out afterwards that he was squirrelling away materials for his own use. I should have known better, I suppose. Eventually we settled on dog shows. It is not unusual for dog owners to turn up at 10 or more shows a year. Perfect disguise. Rallied groups from all over the country.

"I think that the squad is about ready, Sergeant," he boomed. "Big day tomorrow" he said to me, "The Findhorn International Dog Show and Ceilidh. We hope to get a best of breed at least. Good for morale…"

The Colonel was interrupted by the sound of a police Land Rover coming to a halt on the gravel drive. Sergeant Fraser, the driver, parked up – putting on his hat as a sign that he was on official business. The Colonel greeted him warmly, if slightly warily. "Sergeant, what brings you here?"

"Ah Colonel MacPherson, exercising the dogs I see," observed Fraser, taking in the scene.

A distinguished-looking elderly lady was being helped down from the rear of the vehicle by a police constable. She must have been a real visual treat in her younger years with the high cheekbones, piercing blue eyes and that determined jaw.

"I believe that you have lost something Colonel," said Fraser.

"Thank you kindly, Fraser. I see that you have returned the Major."

I was very surprised. So this was Major MacPherson MC, retired infantry officer. Even the Colonel looked impressed as, after carefully adjusting his seams, the Major walked towards us with all the poise and grace of a fashion model.

"Ah, number 87. Countess von Krausdresser – his finest creation."

For his part the Major took in the view. The grey, depressing walls, the grim, featureless towers, the reception committee lined up, just itching for an excuse to unleash their pack of vicious dogs. He recognised the place as Stalag XXI immediately. Funny-looking dogs though – not the usual sort. Perhaps the war was going badly for the Germans and there was a shortage of Alsatians. Or possibly the bigger dogs had all been sent to the Russian Front, leaving the smaller and older ones behind as some kind of home guard – a canine Volksturm.

Taking in our little group the Major observed, "Bagged you as well, have they Colonel. Chin up, I will be forming an escape committee in the infirmary after lights out." And with that he strode majestically towards the house to be greeted by Erik. "Wilkommen, Herr Major." I half expected him to add 'For you Tommy, ze war is over.'

Getting back to business Fraser announced, "I have

some policemen here from London. They're asking about someone called Charles Edward Stuart."

"The name's familiar," mused the Colonel, "what's he done?"

"Apparently he's leading a gang of dangerous terrorists."

The Colonel feigned deafness, a useful affliction that comes and goes as required explained away with the phrase 'The guns, dear boy, the guns.'

"A dangerous gang of tourists, you say. Now there's a thing. We don't see many tourists around here but I shall certainly keep an eye open."

"See that you do, Colonel, see that you do. Here are some pictures of men you should be looking out for," said Fraser handing over several photographs to MacPherson who studied them carefully. I assumed with relief that my portrait was not among them when Fraser asked me "Are you here for the show?"

I nodded in affirmation; keeping silent seemed to be the best thing to do in the circumstances.

"It should be a good show this year. There are entries from as far away as Aberdeen."

"I believe that there may even be some from further south as well," added the Colonel, mischievously.

"Really," responded Fraser, "well I hope that they do not run into the dangerous terrorists." The Sergeant laughed as he strode back to the Land Rover, the Colonel laughing with him.

After the Land Rover had disappeared down the drive, the Colonel showed me the two photographs. "Do you know these two?"

I knew exactly who they were. "DCI Cumberland and DI Monro from Special Branch," I replied. "They have been chasing me."

"Ah, the Rabbie Burns Unit. I thought that we would see them soon enough."

"Why did Sergeant Fraser tell you that they were here? Is he a supporter?"

"Good Lord no, he is just a friend who wants a quiet life. Live and let live is his motto, but he is not keen on superior officers from Nairn yet alone from London."

MacPherson returned to the matter in hand, inviting me to accompany him as Gordon lined the unit up for a final inspection. In proper military fashion he patted heads, adjusted collars – on the dogs as well as the men. I just looked faintly embarrassed.

The dogs were very friendly. The first one had to be held back with some difficulty from jumping up in its enthusiasm to greet me. There was a general whining sound growing in crescendo as we walked down the line, eventually changing to enthusiastic barks. When the first dog got loose, I stood my ground manfully while the handler tried to retrieve the animal. This strategy was abandoned as soon as I realized that the odour of the black pudding in my trouser pocket was the cause of the excitement. The only thing that I could think of was to run, which I did, making for the nearest tree. As I ran, I hurled bannock cakes and black pudding at the dogs, distracting them long enough to be able to climb to safety.

MacPherson and Gordon roared with laughter at my discomfort, although afterwards they told me that it had not occurred to them to use black pudding as a method of distracting dogs, a technique they would put to good use very soon.

FRIDAY AFTERNOON –

A FACE TO BE RECKONED WITH

I spent a pleasant afternoon with Flora, who showed me round the grounds of Brady Castle. I had an uneasy feeling that we were being watched most of the way round, but perhaps this was just understandable paranoia having being chased the length of the country by Cumberland and Monro. I had been provided with a pair of replacement trousers so as not to excite the local dog population once again, the odour of black pudding lingering long after the cause had been devoured. This was my third pair of trousers in three days and if Special Branch would obligingly confine any descriptions and E-Fits of me to the waist and below I could become a master of disguise.

Flora had asked for a picnic tea on the south lawn and by the time we arrived Mrs McGregor had duly obliged. It was only then that I realised how hungry I was, having generously shared my breakfast with a baying pack of Scottie dogs. Just being with Flora had made me forget the needs of the earthly plane; I was in seventh heaven. I worked my way through a generous helping of scones whilst at the same time listening to Flora continuing her historical review of the estate and the MacPherson family. She could have been talking about molecular science for all I cared, the rhythmic lilt of her voice being sufficient to keep me enthralled. I think that we had just reached the twelfth century and Robert the Bastard (he was legitimate – he was just a bastard) when I noticed a face staring out from behind a clump of bamboo. It was an ancient face, so wrinkled and weather-beaten that it could even have been Robert the Bastard checking on the veracity of Flora's recitation. I winked at Flora to attract her attention, with only a slight nod of my head in the direction of the bush. Flora winked back with a 'You are saucy!' expression. I tried again, nodding a bit more vigorously this time.

"You want me to go behind the bamboo bushes with you?" asked Flora with an impish smile.

"No! I mean yes, that would be nice, but the space is already occupied."

"Oh, that's what all the 'come hither' winking was about, and I thought that you fancied me." Flora pretended to be offended and looked coquettishly in the opposite direction.

"Of course I fancy you, and I'd love to discuss this in more detail behind the bush, but there is someone already there, spying on us."

"Of course there is, he's been following us the whole afternoon. He always does; it's nothing personal. I'm flattered that you had not noticed him earlier, you obviously only had eyes for me and so I shall very probably forgive you," she declared with a flourish.

The way the conversation was going the spy was probably P.G. Wodehouse, researching his next Bertie Wooster novel.

"But who the devil is spying on us, old thing?"

"Why it is none other than Kabukazi."

Ah, so it wasn't P.G. Wodehouse after all. Perhaps we could now talk normally.

"You know him then?"

"We don't know his real name, we just call him that. He's been here forever?"

"Kabukazi, doesn't that mean 'divine wind'?"

"No that's Kamikazi, Kabukazi means 'downwind'. Don't ever be downwind of him without a respirator. After a lifetime in the same clothes, there's a bit of an odour."

"But who is he? Why is he here?"

"Uncle says that he's been trying to kill the Major for nearly 50 years, something to do with Malaysia. The Major claims that he was carrying out undercover work during the communist insurgency in 1957 dressed, for some reason that remains a mystery, as a Malay village woman. Kabukazi was still hiding in the jungle refusing to accept that the war was over, and that Japan had officially surrendered. He had been brought up to believe that the Japanese would never surrender and that civilians as well as combatants would rather die than kowtow to the Westerners. The Major and Kabukazi met up somewhere in the jungle south of Penang, we don't know exactly what happened, but it involved severe loss of face for the Japanese soldier. The Colonel believes that Kabukazi stowed away in the Battalion troopship back to Scotland and has been stalking the Major ever since in an attempt to restore his family honour. He never bothers the rest of us and, well… we've all grown rather fond of him."

"And the Major?"

"He can take care of himself. He is usually one step ahead."

By now the face had disappeared, no doubt to search for the Major elsewhere.

"Dinner will be at 19.46," said Flora looking at her watch.

"That is a very precise time."

"It is always at 19.46, after the battle of Culloden – Uncle insists. The Major started the tradition on the 200th Anniversary just after the war, and the Colonel has carried it on ever since. But I have some things that I must do now, so perhaps you could pass the time in the library."

This mystery and intrigue business was becoming very frustrating. Perhaps I should have taken the opportunity with Flora behind the bushes, Japanese soldier or no Japanese soldier. Without a better option, I decided that I would spend some time in the library. It was the sort of room that you would imagine in a stately home, shelves laden with books of all shapes and sizes but with one common denominator. They all seemed in pristine condition, giving the distinct impression that they had not been read by anyone in over two hundred years, that is all apart from some well-thumbed volumes on the Jacobite wars.

I decided that I should do a bit of reading about the '45 Rebellion, to understand why the Colonel was so passionate about it all, and buried myself in an eyewitness account by one James Ray entitled 'A Complete History of the Rebellion. From its first rise, in 1745, to its total suppression in the Glorious Battle of Culloden, in April 1746'. I was so engrossed that I did not at hear the Colonel enter the room.

"You have to remember, that account is biased, laddie."

"Aren't all accounts biased?" I replied. "History is written by the winners after all."

"I suppose you're right," the Colonel conceded.

I thought that this might be a good time to ask Colonel MacPherson what the mystery and intrigue was all about.

"Why is it that you still feel passionately about Culloden after all these years?"

This was a cue for an accompanying 'wee dram'. He poured the usual measures into a pair of whisky glasses and settled down for the explanation.

"Well," he thought for a moment before continuing, "it was the end of Scotland, and Scottish dreams. We are a proud race and to be ruled be Germans for all these years is a continued wound in the Scottish Heart."

"But as I remember it, the Stuarts and the Bruces were both descended from Norman knights, not the Scots."

"Aye that's true, but after centuries of breathing the pure air and drinking the pure water, they could not help but have Scottish blood coursing through their veins."

"So are you planning to create an independent Scotland, like the Scottish National Party?"

"Certainly not," spluttered the Colonel, "we want to create a United Scotland. Those tartan Tories of the SNP care nothing about our proud history, they would sell out the Stuart heritage for control of an oilfield. What happens when the oil runs out?"

"But United with whom?" I was baffled.

"England and Wales of course. As we were until James VII, your James II, was unlawfully removed from the throne, to be followed a Dutchman and then a succession of German Hanoverians."

"But the Scottish Parliament voted for the Act of Union."

"Aye, but only after a mixture of threats and being heavily bribed. And do you know that on the day the Bill came before the English Parliament the matter was considered so unimportant that MPs also had time to discuss an Act for mending roads between the villages of Hockliffe and Woodbourne. An end to 1000 years of History, not with a bang but with a whimper."

"But surely no one else cares?"

"They do. The army in Scotland are with us. The Government have disbanded all the famous regiments – the Argyle and Sutherlanders, the Scottish Borderers, the Gordon Highlanders, the Black Watch and many more. Do you know what they have replaced them with – the Scottish Regiment. It's like saying 'The Scottish play' instead of *Macbeth*, as if even mentioning the name of these once proud regiments whose soldiers once defeated tyranny across the globe, would be to court disaster. Most of the English Regiments that are left feel the same, and they are all pissed off that the Queen allows her army to be sent into battle with inadequate equipment, inadequate training and inadequate Generals. And when our boys and girls are damaged in mind or body, they are sent back home and treated in a hospital room full of geriatrics. What sort of a monarch would allow that? Something has to be done."

"So you are planning to replace the Queen?"

"Aye, and the government. The rightful King will arrive from France in just over two days' time, and we will stage what you might call a coup to place him on his rightful throne. There are many, many groups around the country that will give him their support. Charles Stuart only has to turn up and the wave of support will carry him all the way to London."

"But Special Branch will be covering the major ports and airports, how will he get into the country?"

He had no real need to explain further, I had already guessed. The closest place to France was Deal on the South Coast, and that is presumably where the Prince would arrive. And this is where I had stumbled into the plot in the first place, by being in the wrong place with the right name.

"I believe that I can trust you with this information, but anyway you will be kept with us until after the coup. We are planning for the Prince to land in England in the early hours of Monday morning. A fishing boat will leave Calais during the night and land him on the beach at Deal from where he will be met and taken to London. We have left nothing to chance. Everything is prepared."

"And what is my role in all of this?"

"As an illusion, a deception. The police think that you are the Prince, and so we thought we would encourage them to distract their attention from Deal. By putting Deal Castle under surveillance they very nearly forced us to cancel the whole plan."

"So you're pretending that I'm the Young Pretender?"

"Aye, that's about the size of it."

I realised that I was now implicated in this plot up to my neck, but as beheading was still on the statute books for treason, it probably did not matter if I was implicated further than my neck. Although I was becoming quite fond of the Colonel I was not sure whether he was completely loony or extremely clever.

"And the ceilidh and dog show, is that all deception?"

"Maybe, maybe not. We are having a final briefing of the senior cadres in the afternoon. But we will just have to keep an eye out with Special Branch around; Cumberland and Monro." He chuckled to himself.

"What's so funny?" I asked.

The Colonel walked across to a huge panorama on the wall, which I assumed must be a painting of Culloden.

"Cuil Lodair," he sighed, "Culloden to the Sassenachs. You see the line of Redcoats, and behind them this group on horses." I nodded affirmatively. "That," he indicated a mounted figure on the painting, "is the Duke of Cumberland, and in the first line of Redcoats here, the pivotal point of the whole battle, is Colonel Monro's Regiment. Cumberland and Monro, I think that the policemen have no idea what those names mean around here. Of all the officers they could have sent. The irony of it all; there are many around here that would despatch these two and push their bodies into the Firth without so much as a backward glance."

"Why don't they?"

"Because Special Branch might replace them with somebody competent."

I looked closer at the tableau. It was so full of detail that it was possible to make out individual tartans on the figures, charging forlornly at the solid red wall.

"And where are the Macphersons in this picture?"

The Colonel pulled himself up to his full height, chest out, as if to emphasise the importance of his reply.

"We were not there." There was a tear in his eye as he made the confession. "Cluny MacPherson and his men had been ordered to defend Inverness from the south, in the Badenoch, our homeland. The only MacPherson present was 'Black' Jack MacPherson who was a Bagpiper with Lord George Murray."

"And where is he on the picture?"

"He's not, by this time he was dead. Before the battle got under way he stood out in front of the Scottish Line playing 'MacPherson's Lament' to encourage the troops, only to be hit by at least three musket balls within seconds. Funny thing, I've studied the contemporary maps and he was out of range of the English troops. It remains a mystery to this day; must have been a stray bullet."

So the only MacPherson to be present had been shot by music lovers from his own side.

"I would dearly like to have been there on that sad and famous day; to take part in a real Highland Charge brandishing cold steel. Had the MacPhersons been there on the day then I am sure that the outcome would have been very different. Cumberland and Monro would not have repelled the MacPherson clan." The Colonel continued to look at the painting wistfully. After a while he topped up both our glasses and changed the subject.

"I was sorry about your cat by the way, what was its name again?"

"Lawrence."

"Ah yes, the first casualty of the Jacobite Rebellion. Perhaps he will become famous like Horst Wessel in Nazi Germany. He became immortal after a song was written about him."

"But Horst Wessel died in a street brawl."

"The Nazis created a legend out of it nevertheless. Just imagine; we could do the same. We could… we could have a statue of Lawrence on the fourth plinth in Trafalgar Square."

I had to accept that Lawrence would be extremely pleased with that. He could spend eternity pretending not to notice the pigeons pecking away beneath him. I could see the pose that the sculptor would adopt, Lawrence had this way of pretending he was not really there or, if he was there that he did not really care about some silly birds. I could swear that sometimes I heard him whistling nonchalantly, as he slowly ambled in the direction of any feathered creature that had foolishly sought food in Lawrence's chosen killing zone.

Flora had entered the library towards the end of this discussion and took the opportunity of the pause to announce that it was time for dinner. She gave me a wink before saying, "You're not still gabbing are you, Uncle? Keeping poor Charles from his dinner." she laughed. "There will be plenty of opportunities to complain about the dastardly English and Hanoverians later. It's very nearly 19.46."

"I am sorry, my dear. I was forgetting myself. Lead on."

I was growing quite fond of the Colonel, but I could not decide whether or not he was as mad as a hatter.

FRIDAY NIGHT –

'ONE POTATO' AND A CASSEROLE

The dining room was typical of the rest of the house with heavy oak panelling, dark Victorian furniture and solemn-looking drapes and curtains. The resultant gloom was offset by a splendid Edwardian chandelier, which brilliantly lit the dining table while leaving patches of shadow in the corners. As we entered one such patch came suddenly to life, which rather startled me. It was Mrs McGregor topping up her gloomy quotient. She was the sort of person who smiled first thing in the morning so as to get it over with and concentrate on the day ahead. As she moved into the lighted area she gave me such a malevolent stare that I could only assume that she had been practising all afternoon.

"And where would you like me to sit, Mrs McGregor?" I enquired politely.

"Where the mats are laid," was the self-evident reply delivered as a withering put-down. I could see that our relationship was developing well.

Lady MacPherson, who had bounced into the room just behind us, answered the question.

"You must sit here next to me, so that I can hear all about you."

Still an attractive woman, she must have been a stunner in her youth. She had red hair similar to Flora's, and with the same sparkling eyes and sing-song voice. She had a perfect ski-slope nose; when I later remarked on this the Colonel agreed and said this was appropriate as she was 'piste' most of the time. Age had added voluptuous curves that would have been much admired by the 17th century Stuart monarchs. They liked their women to be on the large side. Even her husband was not sure of her age. He remembered her having a 49th birthday party quite a few years ago, but since then she had steadfastly ignored any such anniversary, which spared him the tedious business of having to buy her a card. Lady Ann therefore remained 49 to this day and maintain this fiction by occasionally suggesting she would like to hold a party on her next birthday.

"It is one of my specials tonight," said Lady Ann "Beef in Red Wine with Dauphinoise Potatoes, I love cooking with wine."

"She cooks a lot with red wine," suggested Flora.

"And occasionally with food," added the Colonel.

"Stuff and nonsense, Angus. More red wine anybody?" she enquired and without looking up for a response, topped up her own glass closely followed by mine. My protest that I had already had too much to drink was met by a 'don't be silly'.

Flora was placed on the other side of me opposite the Colonel, leaving one place unfilled.

"Is the Major joining us tonight?" asked Flora.

"He's around somewhere," was the reply. "I've asked Erik to try and find him."

"We had better start without him then," declared Lady MacPherson nodding towards Mrs McGregor, who with a 'Yes Ma'am' disappeared into the kitchen.

"She does not seem to be a very happy lady," I observed.

"Never been the same since she lost her husband, our gardener," replied the Colonel adding, "she often tries to contact him though a professional medium, but no luck so far."

"That explains things. When did he die?"

"Oh no, he hasn't died," interjected Lady MacPherson, "he ran off to Stirling with Jean, our chambermaid. Mrs McGregor just wants to find an address so that she can go round there, rolling pin in hand, to have a full and frank exchange of views. I've seen her practising on one of the suits of armour when she thinks that I am not looking."

I decided to be even more wary of the housekeeper, a scary woman indeed. She quickly returned with plates of soup and a pannier of bread rolls, one of which carefully landed in my lap with all the precision of a Tomahawk missile. "Sorry," she muttered while ensuring that no more than half of my soup was spilt onto the placemat.

"Do you have anything I can use to mop up this soup," I asked politely.

"You'll not be getting another bread roll until you've eaten that one. And anyway, gentleman don't dunk," and with that admonishment she turned on her heels and disappeared back into the kitchen.

The Colonel laughed, "I think that she's taken a fancy to you. You'd better keep your door locked tonight."

I didn't think that a locked door would be an obstacle to Mrs McGregor!

"How long are you staying with us? You will come to the Ceilidh won't you?" said Lady Ann, "I shall be performing a piece."

"Oh, really what instrument do you play?" I enquired politely.

"I am a modest performer on the piano," she replied modestly. "I studied under Sir John Barbaroli at the Barbican. He was inspirational. But if you will excuse me, I must go and assist Mrs McGregor. Don't go away will you, young man."

Making sure his wife was out of earshot, the Colonel continued the story.

"Technically she did do most of her studying under Sir John – he lived in the flat above. He kept complaining about the noise to the landlords but they took no action. One evening, as Ann was practising a rather difficult passage for the 27th time, he stormed downstairs and rang the doorbell. Ann answered the door to find Sir John on her doorstep in a pair of red pyjamas, his face a matching bright red with anger. "Madame," he said "when Beethoven wrote his Piano Sonata in A Flat he was referring to the key signature, not a location." Pushing past, he sat down at the keyboard and demonstrated the correct way to play the tricky passage, knocked off the rest of the sonata, threw in the same composer's 'Appasionata' for good measure, hammering on the keys as if was exorcising some form of demon, and finished off with a quick transcription of 'Leaving on a Jet Plane.' "Madame," he said, "may I wish you a good day, a good night and a goodbye. I have sold my flat and I am now departing these shores. And if you have an ounce of humanity in your body, may I please, please ask you to shoot this piano and put it out of its misery!" And with that stormed off to complete his packing. Ann insists, that however brief, this counts as tuition from the great man!"

Lady Ann returned and pronounced, "The stew will be coming presently. Now where were we, oh yes, the ceilidh. I shall be playing 'Farewell to Stromness' by Maxwell Davies. I find that tune always haunts me."

"I am not surprised it haunts you," said the Colonel, "you have murdered it often enough."

"Stuff and nonsense. And I suppose that you are going to be strangling a few more cats for our musical pleasure."

"I shall of course be playing the famous 'MacPherson's Lament' on the bagpipes. It's the traditional way to finish the Ceilidh.

"We finish with it because it is a sign to all music lovers to go home! Thank goodness for the European Union, I say."

"Why is that?" I asked.

"Noise pollution. They have set a limit on noise decibels, which is a bit of problem for bagpipe players. Poor old Angus will have to perform his 'death of a moggie' requiem from a boat moored in the bay. And if the boat sinks he can always use the pipes as a snorkel!"

"Auntie, Uncle," interjected Flora. "I am sure our guest does not want to hear your squabbles about music."

Actually, I did. I found the interplay between the two of them fascinating. The continuing argument was interrupted only when Mrs McGregor announced that the main course was now ready. Lady Ann and Flora followed her into the kitchen but soon returned with the casserole and the potatoes. Mrs McGregor arrived with a bowl of green beans, which she proceeded to hurl in the general direction of my plate.

"Would you be wanting any more beans?" she enquired.

"No thank you, I can always use the ones in my lap if I'm hungry."

The conversation slowed as we tucked into what was an excellent dish, the gaps in eating filled only by the chink of wine glasses being replenished.

The Colonel had noticed me examining my wine glass which had images of roses etched onto the sides.

"I see that you have noticed the Jacobite symbols on the wine glass. That was a practice that sprang up after 1746, so that supporters could identify each other. We have continued to this day, although it is hardly a secret any more." He raised his glass for a toast, "To Charles Edward Stuart, the Prince over the Water and the rightful King."

Flora and Lady Ann joined in, leaving me to consider which side I was on. It was an easy decision. I had no particular desire to overthrow the Government, except by voting of course, and rebellions usually involved some kind of physical violence. I was definitely not in favour of that and said so.

"Ah but this will be a relatively peaceful coup. Everything is set. We have infiltrated English Heritage and will be able to seize all the strongpoints in the south in a matter of minutes, Dover, Salisbury, Newcastle and many more. It was a strategic error on the part of the government to place all of these places in the hands of a few little old ladies in the gift shops. I don't think that they will hold out for long. And we have plans to infiltrate 5,000 of our men and women into the centre of London without being detected."

"And how do you propose to do that, in giant pigeon costumes?" I said jokingly.

The Colonel's brow furrowed, "Who told you that? That is indeed part of our plan. This is serious, please do not leak this to anyone else."

"Or Uncle's men will have to peck you to death," added Flora facetiously. "Once we have presented Charles in the Houses of Parliament as the rightful King, the support will be overwhelming."

"But how do you know that he is the rightful King. How do you know that it is not me, or anyone else with the surname Stuart?"

I was slightly offended when Flora burst out laughing. "You don't even look like a king. No offence, you have lots of good qualities but I can't see you sitting on the Stone of Scone without fidgeting and demanding a cushion." The joyful sight of Flora laughing was more than enough to compensate for the comment.

"Besides," said the Colonel, "there is an heirloom held by my family for generations. One half of a brooch that was given to Cluny MacPherson after Culloden. It has an inscription, which reads:

'Whosoever, the other half bring,
Will be your only lawful King.'

I am sure that our man is the King, I have seen the other half of the brooch."

I felt a little foolish. It was easy not to take the Colonel seriously, but he was clearly very committed to the plan of rebellion. The details I had heard so far might seem far-fetched and ridiculous, with as many flaws as a multistorey car park, but the Colonel was perhaps just mad enough to make it work.

"If you are coming tomorrow you will have to come in disguise, we do not want Cumberland or Monro hauling you off to spill the beans, which remands me, you will need a replacement pair of trousers after Mrs McGregor's handiwork. Or better still, I will find you a kilt to wear for tomorrow, which should help to fool Special Branch."

Lady Ann joined in, "I shall make sure to remove his trousers tonight Angus, leave it to me. I shall look forward to it."

"Were you troubled by strange noises last night?" asked Lady MacPherson.

"I wasn't troubled by anything last night, I was dead to the world. What strange noises?"

"Other people dead to the world. Ghosts, family ghosts. We have a few present here."

"My favourite is James Macpherson," ventured the Colonel. "Lost his head in the Civil War and has been looking for it ever since. Unlikely to find it on account of the fact that he cannot see very well, or in fact at all."

"But James never goes upstairs, Angus," replied Lady Ann. "He can't find his way upstairs; just wanders around downstairs bumping into things. Anyway, if you do see a ghost they are almost all harmless."

I was about to seek clarification about the ghosts that were not harmless when there was a sudden banging at the door. As the door was opened there was a through draught from the dining room window, and I felt a cold shiver down my spine. At the same time a cold clammy object was slowly moving along my knee. I am not sure whether I was relieved or not to that it was Lady Ann's hand.

The banging was from Sergeant Gordon. "Begging your pardon, sir." he said after putting his head round the door. "Erik has asked me to inform you that they have not yet recaptured the Major, but that they think they know where he is."

"Very good Sergeant. I am sure that Erik and his team will track him down before he gets out of the grounds again."

The Colonel took this as an opportunity to end the evening's entertainment especially as Lady Ann had suggested that she play for us on the piano.

"I have an early start in the morning so if you will forgive me, I will turn in. How about you dear?" he asked Lady Ann.

"I shall help Mrs McGregor with the tidying up, and I have a few other things that I should do first."

Flora also made her excuses to retire, which gave me my cue to follow her upstairs, which I did after bidding the usual goodnights to the dinner guests. We reached her bedroom first and I was rewarded outside with a goodnight kiss. "After all," said Flora, "I might never see you again if Auntie's ghosts get you. In fact I might have to check up on you later to see if you are still alive."

I made my way to my own room with a light heart and with the proverbial skip in my walk. I had hardly been inside for more than a minute, when there was a knock at the door. Assuming that it must be Flora, I put on what I thought was a sultry voice, but it probably came over like a camp Lauren Bacall. I coughed in a suggestive way and said, "I'm ready for you now," although the cough got out of hand and ran into the vocals.

Colonel MacPherson looked puzzled as he entered the room. "Are you all right laddie, you sounded a bit strange. In fact you sounded a bit like that famous actress from the forties."

"Lauren Bacall?"

"No, a much smaller person altogether. Let me see now. Ah yes, lassie, that's it. Anyway, I've brought you your clothes for tomorrow. I'll leave them here, shall I? As long as you're sure you're all right. You should think about getting that throat seen to though."

"I'm quite all right, thank you." It was so embarrassing.

After I was certain that the door was closed, I took off my food-stained trousers and placed them carefully on the chair, to be dealt with in the morning. I had just taken off the rest of the clothes and was admiring my body in the mirror, face on, holding my breath, which miraculously made the paunch disappear, when there was another knock on the door. I hoped that it would be Flora but, after the last visitor, I decided that I had better play safe, taking the trousers from the chair to cover my nakedness.

116

"Come in."

"I'm here to collect your trousers for washing," said Lady MacPherson. "Oh, you seem to be expecting me, you sweet young man." And with that she ripped the trousers out of my hands.

I then experienced my second goodnight kiss, although Lady MacPherson's was far less delicate. Her manoeuvre was accomplished by pulling me towards her with both hands on my buttocks, and with a playful squeezing of my genitals.

"I shall place these in the wash straight away," she declaimed, "and then nothing can come between us." This was all said in a dramatic voice as if to emphasise her departure from the room. I was slightly concerned that it also foretold her return. I hoped that Flora would arrive first, and climbed into bed to await her arrival. The red wine and the fresh air that day had tired me out and, within half an hour, I was dozing off thinking about apparitions.

I am not afraid of ghosts, as far as I am aware. This had not always been the case as I, like most children, would be traumatised by my parents with the threat of the Bogeyman getting hold of me if I did not go get into bed/clean my teeth/ stop talking after the light was out… well for pretty much anything really. The Bogeyman ran a strict regime, although he clearly mellowed with age and, after I was about 9, he did not bother to call at all. Come to think of it, this was pretty much at the same time as Father Christmas stopped calling, with my parents having to do all the work on Christmas Eve. There was no explanation for this sudden change. My parents, avid *Mail* readers, often talked about immigrants and how the government should stop them coming into the country. I assumed that as Father Christmas was from Lapland and the Bogeyman was from Outer Mongolia, that they had both been deported for not having a work permit. However in the early years, while the Bogeyman was in the country, I would often hide with the blankets dragged up towards my chin and the pillow over my head so that I could not be seen.

In later years I assumed that the phenomenon of ghosts was explained by the wind, reflected lights, structural movements and too much alcohol. It was no coincidence that these ghosts were generally located in old buildings, representing poor souls from centuries earlier who had come to an untimely end in a variety of unfortunate ways. On the basis of the Colonel's stories there would be an army of long-dead MacPhersons wandering about with missing limbs, heads, or in some cases, bodies. Perhaps I should keep an eye out and a spare pillow handy, just in case. Then I thought that 'keeping an eye out' was just the sort of thing that that might attract a visually challenged apparition. I decided to keep both eyes in under the protective custody of my eyelids.

Dozing fitfully, I was brought to attention by the sound of the bedroom door slowly opening. Anxiously waiting to see which branch of the ancestral line would assail me first, I was startled to see a shadowy outline of a figure entirely draped in white cotton, the classic ghost costume. The door was shut more rapidly than it had been opened and, with the lack of light from the landing such as it was, it was impossible to make out any details, although I could hear the apparition making its way slowly towards me.

"Are you awake, Charles?"

I breathed a sigh of relief – it was Flora.

"I wish you wouldn't frighten me like that," I protested.

"Scared of ghosts are we? Don't listen to my aunt, there are no such things," laughed Flora climbing on to the bed and, with the cover over her head, she whooaa'd a few times in her no doubt highly accurate rendition of a MacPherson family ghost.

"There are a lot of things that I did not believe in a few days ago."

"Such as?"

"That I would be sharing a bed with a beautiful young woman like you before the week was out, for one."

"Flattery will get you everywhere," promised Flora, taking off her nightdress as she did so. I could feel her soft warm body as we cuddled up. This branch of the extended family definitely had all her body parts intact – I checked.

"This is nice," came the soft, sleepy bedtime voice.

Despite the threatened march past of the entire MacPherson dynasty, I was determined not to be distracted from the potential of the situation. I felt the blood coursing in to various parts of my anatomy as I caressed Flora. We exchanged kisses, slowly at first and then more passionately.

(Don't get your hopes up – The Editor)

"What's that?" said Flora in alarm.

"It's my wedding tackle," I answered, using a description that in my case was largely inappropriate.

"Not that, stupid, I thought I could hear a sound."

All I could hear was my heart racing and the sound of my expectations being dashed.

"There it is again. It's coming from the fireplace."

This time I could also hear sounds of movement coming from the other side of the fireplace.

"I'm sorry I made fun of you. If it is a ghost, then I'm worried that I'll scream and wake Auntie Ann up. I'm more worried about Auntie discovering us than a ghost. The ghost would be gone in the morning but Auntie will very definitely be here, and she doesn't approve of this sort of thing outside of marriage," confessed Flora. My wife hadn't approved of this sort of thing inside marriage either.

"Hide under the bedclothes and put something in your mouth to stop yourself screaming, if you think it necessary. I'll let you know when it's safe to come out again."

Burrowing under the sheets, Flora did just that, but the result was not at all as I had expected. I thought a knuckle, or the corner of a pillow would suffice, not a temporarily prominent part of my anatomy. At another time, in another place, I am sure the experience would have been very pleasurable, but hardly the way to greet your first ghost. As the noise from the fireplace came ever nearer, Flora tightened her grasp. My eyes began to water as the tension in her hands and lips increased until eventually I was not sure who would come first, the ghost or myself.

A shadowy figure emerged from the fireplace and into the bedroom, which was now bathed in moonlight, the clouds having temporarily passed over.

"Is the coast clear?" asked a voice that I recognised instantly, as did Flora because I felt the pressure relax in the nick of time. It was the Major.

"What on earth are you doing?" I enquired.

"Need-to-know basis only," replied the Major, "don't want you blurting everything out under torture." He obviously had no idea what I had just been going through. With a wink, he crossed the room and disappeared through the massive oak wardrobe that occupied the entire wall in the other side of the bedroom.

Flora emerged from her hiding place, asking, "What was he doing up here?"

"I don't know. Perhaps he is building a glider in the attic as they did in Colditz. But what were you doing down there?"

"Exactly as you said. Anyway he's gone now; perhaps we could carry on from where we left off." And with that she put her arms around me with a little squeeze showing her relief. As we settled down once more, there was, inevitably, another sound from behind the fireplace and this time the apparition made its presence felt before Flora could disappear with her comfort object.

Erik emerged, and on seeing the two of us, stood to attention with the usual clicking of heels.

"Ah Mr Charles and Fraulein Flora. I am sorry to disturb you. Did the Major pass this way?"

I nodded in confirmation.

"Das Gut. In which case I need disturb you no longer." And with that he blew on a whistle, which was hanging round his neck for just such a purpose. As he did so he turned towards the fireplace with a guttural call of "Raus, Raus." Three men in combat fatigues with German shepherd dogs, straining at the leash, emerged from the fireplace and were ushered across to the oak wardrobe, disappearing inside hot on the heels of the Major. The dogs were slipping and sliding on the wooden floor in their eagerness to pursue. Erik clicked his heels once again and with a cheery "Guten Abend" followed the others, closing the wardrobe door behind him.

Flora and I looked at each other and burst out laughing, relieving the tension. Although embarrassing, this was clearly nothing to be frightened of. There was almost immediately another noise from the fireplace, this time accompanied by an indescribable smell that could very easily emanate from the putrefied body of Robert the Bastard. I found it unnerving but Flora seemed to be strangely unperturbed. The latest passer-by entered the room in a crouched posture, blinking in the moonlight. He was wearing a jungle-green uniform, although the colour had faded over the years, one of those forage caps with a sun curtain protecting the neck, and ragged puttees wrapped around a pair of battered brown leather boots. He was carrying a bolt-action rifle topped with a vicious-looking bayonet that glinted in the moonlight. I recognised the uniform as that of a Japanese Imperial Army Corporal circa 1945. And why not, if the Major thought the war still going on, why should he be alone in that view? Adjusting his eyes to the light, the Corporal was momentarily startled to see that the room was already occupied. He stood to attention before bowing politely. I pointed towards the wardrobe, a gesture that he acknowledged by nodding back and bowing once again. With that he resumed his crouching position and disappeared into the wardrobe, his bayonet leading the way. I recognised the wizened old face with bottle-rimmed glasses as Kabukazi, the man I had seen earlier in the garden. Flora had recognised the smell.

What was it with this bedroom? Was it a registered footpath? A right of way established centuries ago? What would be next, a farmer taking his sheep to market? Lord Lucan riding Shergar? Elvis? Or, if Elvis wasn't dead, then perhaps some of his thousands of impersonators would stage a carousing march past in silver-sequined hipsters. Or perhaps it would be a gaggle of pilgrims following the trail of Saint Ramsey, who had famously, and within living memory, cleared the Findhorn Zoological Gardens of snakes, much to the annoyance of the Reptile House keeper. The answer was not long in coming. The clouds had returned, once more obscuring the light of the moon and plunging the room into darkness, broken only by a shaft of yellow light emerging from under the wardrobe door. I almost expected a dramatic organ peal as the wardrobe door was opened and the bright light exploded into the bedroom.

"Have you seen the Major?" enquired Sergeant Gordon, for it was he.

I pointed back the way he came and with a "Sorry to disturb you," he was gone, the room returning to an inky black. For several minutes nothing else happened and I hoped desperately that the evening's light entertainment was now over, and that the prospect of serious work with Flora could at last get underway.

However, almost immediately, there was the unmistakeable sound of the bedroom doorknob being slowly twisted from the outside. The bedroom door briefly opened, but I was not able to make out who had entered before the closing door blotted out the dim light from the landing. Flora had been fairly relaxed about the last few visitors, but fear of the unknown had again forced her under the covers, and I could feel her grip on her comfort object steadily tightening.

Slow, deliberate footsteps made their way to the bed and, still unable to see who it was, I called out. "Who's there?" There was no immediate answer but I could feel someone, or something, climbing under the bedclothes, rapidly followed by the pressure of another hand on my vital organ, resting on top of Flora's. I was the subject of an erotic game of 'One potato, two potato'.

"I see that you were expecting me," said a voice that was instantly recognisable. Flora thought so too.

"Auntie?"

"Flora!!"

I wasn't afraid of ghosts but nevertheless, I could not help but close my eyes, putting a pillow over my head in the hope that the bogeyman would not get me.

SATURDAY MORNING –

DOGGED PURSUIT

I was the last down to breakfast once again. This time my sloth was not induced by alcohol, but by lack of sleep. After all the comings and goings I had slept fitfully, my slumber disturbed by a succession of weird dreams. In one, I dreamt that a naked Lady MacPherson was chasing me across the croquet lawn watched, if such a thing was possible, by a number of headless MacPhersons who were playing croquet using their own heads as balls. I tried to replace these visions with nice thoughts about Flora but whenever I tried, all I could focus on was a pair of bicycle clips. What these had to do with Flora, I had no idea.

Searching in vain for my trousers I remembered that today was the day that I was to give my knees their annual outing, usually performed in the sunny South of France, but on this occasion to be exposed to the full horrors of the North Scotland climate. Putting on the whole kit and caboodle and felling pretty stupid, I looked myself up and down in the mirror. The red hairpiece I was expected to wear made me look remarkably like 'Animal' from the Muppets, or more likely his distant cousin 'Macanimal'.

The Colonel had mentioned that there would probably be Arbroath Smokies for breakfast – a kind of slowly smoked fish. As I entered the dining room Mrs McGregor was bustling about clearing plates away; on seeing me she frowned and pointed to a seat at the end of the table.

"How's the haddock?" I enquired.

Mrs McGregor was disarmed by what she thought was a sudden interest in her health. Rubbing her forehead she said "A little better, thank you. There's black pudding, and I might be able to find you an egg." She was obviously softening.

"Poached?" I asked hopefully.

"No, it'll be from our own hens."

Looking at the cutlery, I asked politely "Is there any chance of a fork?"

Mrs McGregor's face went a bright red, as did mine after she had slapped it extremely hard. "What kind of a woman do you think I am? You think that you can come here with your smooth talk; I could see that you were up to no good last night. First you had your evil way with wee young Flora, and then you set about ruining the reputation of the Mistress and her without a stain on her character. Not content with that you… you… sex fiend, you proposition me in my own dining room. You should be ashamed of yourself. There's black pudding," she said pointing to the side table, "and no egg," and with that she stormed off slamming the door behind her. It seemed pointless to suggest that, as far as I

126

was aware, I had not, unfortunately, had my 'evil way' with anybody since before my marriage. As for the lack of stains on Lady MacPherson's character they might well have been balanced out by the stains on her bed linen, if fate and Flora had not intervened.

After the usual attempt to eat a hearty meal of black pudding and bannock cake, I wondered outside to see what was going on. Nothing was the answer; the place was deserted. I had heard revving of engines at first light and clearly the Colonel and his men had left early, perhaps for some last minute rehearsals on site. After all, as well as the overthrow of the Government and the Monarchy, and the re-establishment of the Stuarts, there was a 'Best of Breed' at stake.

I wondered around the garden for a while, conscious that Kabukazi keeping an eye on me from the safety of the undergrowth. After some time I was rewarded by the appearance of Flora coming out from the South Terrace patio doors. She waved cheerfully to my Japanese stalker, and I swear that the bushes rustled back as an acknowledgement.

"There you are Charles. Did you sleep well? I hope that nobody bothered you."

"Unfortunately nobody did," I replied.

Flora laughed. "Don't be silly, there will be more time for that sort of thing later. We will be having a busy few days."

That was a rallying cry for a revolution, I thought, *Liberty, Equality and more time for sex with Flora.*

"You look awfully fine in your outfit, just like a proper Highlander. With a broadsword in one hand and a target in the other, you could have come straight from the battlefield of Culloden."

Puffed up by this I enquired, "And what famous clan am I representing? Perhaps Macbeth?"

"Oh, that's Smith. You can get tartans for any names these days."

Deflated by this, and thinking that Flora was making a joke, I then reminded that of a front page story of some months ago. A certain Mr. Dunlop from Phoenix, Arizona was furious to find out that the so-called family tartan that he was sold was in fact of the 'Macintyre' clan. The defence was 'Och, everyone knows that Dunlop have been 'makin tyres' for years.'

"We had better get going, Mr Smith," advised Flora.

"Right you are. Who is driving us?" I asked.

"I am. All of the Landrovers went out early this morning. Is there a problem?"

I was a little bit concerned, not because I was worried about Flora's driving although it could be pretty hair-raising, but I was about to be a pillion driver in a kilt. I the event it was not as bad as I had feared, at least to start with. But once out of the grounds Flora started to accelerate. I was desperately holding onto her waist with one hand, trying to make sure my false hair did not come off with the second, whilst holding down the kilt with the third. As obviously I did not have a third, the inevitable happened. The onrushing air generated by the passage of the motorbike, roaring towards Findhorn, created sufficient lift to raise the kilt entirely. I gave the impression of a Whirling Dervish rather than a fierce Highlander,

My very own 'Seven Year Itch 'moment occurred just as we were passing the 'Crown and Usurper, public house, situated on the road between Castle Brady and Findhorn. I was greeted with a rapturous reception from the ladies of the Berwick Women's Institute, who were stopping there for lunch on a tour of the Highlands. Some of them responded in kind. (If you do not want to know the result, look away now-Editor.) The line of colourful underwear had a very familiar look to it, not that I was familiar with women's underwear. It was only further down the road did I realize that the patterns were semaphore and spelt out Nelson's message from Trafalgar-'England Expects Every Man to Do His Duty, Quite what that duty might be, I could only hazard a guess. Mine, by contrast, only conveyed the message 'Marks and Spencer'.

The only way in to Findhorn by road was on the B9011. There was of course the ferry to Nairn, but the new owner soon discovered that he was seasick and would not venture out into the Firth. Instead, he took ramblers on short trips to the other side of the estuary, provided that the weather was fine, but still insisted on wearing the full Captain's regalia, smoking a pipe that omitted more smoke than the Queen Mary, and propping up the bar at the Rebel and Gibbet, telling tall stories of his days at sea for the benefit of tourists. The telephone only worked intermittently as it relied on an old-fashioned switch exchange. This appeared to be manned entirely by members of the Findhorn Swingers who were often called away to make connections of a different sort. Apart from Ouija boards, the only other way of communicating was a tramp in the sand dunes between

Findhorn and Kinloss. For a small fee, the tramp was willing to take a letter or small package to the neighbouring village.

We were eventually welcomed into the Village of Findhorn by a splendid sign, ornamented with paintings of seagulls and fishing boats over stylised waves rippling on a blue background. The sign said 'Findhorn Welcomes Careful Drivers' and immediately written underneath was 'Dead End'. If that was to happen to the careful drivers, what was in store for the reckless? The next sign was 'Findhorn – Twinned with Kinloss'. I turned to Flora, "Isn't that…"

"Yes," responded Flora anticipating the question, "that's the village next to Findhorn. We used to be twinned with a place just outside Oslo, but the miserly Council thought the cost of exchanges was too much. Now the visits are done with bicycles."

"Isn't that's a bit parochial?"

Flora bristled. "We do still have international relations you know, we are official Nodding Acquaintances with Denmark and have exchanged hostages with Iceland."

I was still trying to figure this one out as the motorbike rattled its way down the road into Findhorn, we were bumped this way and that, hanging on for dear life; all apart from one stretch of road where speed bumps had been installed and drivers were warned repeatedly about 'uneven road surfaces'. These had recently been installed with great care; new tarmac carefully laid over the old road surface. It was in fact the best bit of road anywhere between Forres and Inverness, as smooth as a baby's bottom as Alex put it. The further irony was that the new section of 'sleeping policemen' forewarned by the road sign was immediately outside the Findhorn police station in an apt reminder of the usual state of affairs inside.

The village reminded me of the stereotype sets used in cowboy movies. The Rebel and Gibbet public house was immediately opposite the police station, indicating drunks could be forcibly thrown out of the pub and be arrested before they hit the ground on the other side of the road. I was assured that this only happened on Thursdays, pension day at the post office. I had never been to a dog show and neither had I had any desire to take Lawrence to a cat show. Were there shows for other types of pets, I wondered. A show for rodents perhaps, with a prize for the most animals that could sleep on top of each other in a gerbil acrobatic team. Or were there devoted snake owners out there somewhere, leading their pets slithering on the end of a piece of string before being telling them to 'Sit.' If there were I am sure that they could not possibly rival dog owners in their dedication and energy.

The main marquee and a number of satellite marquees were teeming with dogs and their owners. The former were reasonably well behaved but the owners were tense, nervous and irritable. I was staggered by the number of people wandering about with merchandise of all kinds, loaded up with foodstuffs and delicacies from this canine supermarket. I had not appreciated the amount of money that could be spent on a pet. Lawrence had been content with a bowl of dried cat food, lightly garnished with the occasional dead mouse. He would rather drink from puddles than touch the weird chemical concoction from the East Surrey Water Company that I occasionally placed in front of him. On such occasions he would give me a mournful look as if to ask what had he done to deserve a slow lingering death by poisoning. And I do not recall him ever suggesting that he might need a furry overcoat, wellingtons or padded boots. The one thing that I am sure that he would have approved of, a bulletproof vest, did not appear to be on sale.

I was dressed like an extra from 'Braveheart' – false ginger hair and beard, tam-o'-shanter and a blue jacket over a white shirt, not forgetting the kilt with sporran. I certainly looked the part as Flora had confirmed, but I still felt as inconspicuous as a nun on a polar ice cap unless, of course, she was crouching behind the other penguins. But I would caution anyone about wearing a kilt to a dog show. It was worse than wearing a kilt on a motorbike! A multitude of cold nostrils investigating whether Scotsmen really did wear anything underneath the kilt was not a pleasurable experience. One particular slavering Labrador even gave me an 'I thought so, wimp' look before wandering off to tell the others. I came across PC Hawkins with a dog that I recognised by the bits of trouser leg still in its teeth. The disguise did its job as Hawkins walked straight past me, but the dog stopped momentarily until pulled away by its handler. I could tell from the expression on its face that it was only giving me the benefit of the doubt on this occasion. The appearance of my knees had either confused or frightened it. I was not sure which.

Cumberland, Monro and the other Special Branch Officers blended in as best they could. Cumberland had reasoned that to not look out of place at a dog show, one needed a dog. Fraser had been despatched to find a number of these animals at short notice so as to maintain cover, and incredibly he succeeded. He had also entered them for various ring events as instructed. The plan was to have at least one officer, if not more, in the ring at any one time. This way they could have a good look at the other dog handlers. After the first such event Monro rounded on Fraser furiously.

"Are you taking the piss, or what?"

Fraser defended himself, "It was difficult to find suitable dogs at short notice. I had to put up reward notices to come up with anything at all."

"But a Pekinese. That's not a dog, just a cat with a personality problem. I have never been so embarrassed in my life, going round with... this thing on a lead. It was like parading with a Muppet on a stick. What else have you got?"

"Well, there is the little Jack Russell Terrier, name of Twiglet. I am told that it should do well in the obedience testing," ventured Fraser but without much conviction.

"You've got to be joking." Monro's voice grew louder as he remonstrated with Fraser, eventually causing Twiglet to start yelping with excitement before sinking its teeth into the detective's ankle.

"F*ck," exclaimed Monro. Fraser noted surprisingly that on hearing this, the Jack Russell sat obediently down, tongue out, content.

"I think he responded to that," observed Fraser, his words partly obscured by a tannoy announcement. "That's the call for the obedience event now."

"Oh, sh*t," exclaimed Monro, at which point Twiglet

rolled over feigning sleep. Fraser was as surprised as Monro that, with a few other choice words, the Jack Russell was capable of delivering the whole dog repertoire. Fraser was even more surprised when checking his list of animals that Twiglet belonged to the wife of the Reverend Wild. He would look on her with renewed respect at the next vicarage tea party.

DC Munro went on and had an excellent round, with carefully timed shouts of C*nt, F*ck, Ar*e and Sh*t, each producing the required response from the dog, if not the audience. Mothers hurried their children away, covering their children's ears as they did so. DCI Cumberland looked on, open-mouthed with horror. In his view, this was not how to conduct an undercover operation. The Judges could find nothing in the rulebook to disqualify Munro and Twiglet and, even after deducting maximum points for bad language; they were still the clear winners.

Lady MacPherson was gallantly helped on to the awards stand to award the pair the Lord Turette's Memorial Trophy.

Monro approached the stand proudly and on the command 'F*ck', Twiglet sat down as good as gold.

Cumberland suddenly arrived, dusting himself down from the ring. "I've never been so humiliated. Monro, is this your idea of a joke?"

"No Gov. It was all we could get at short notice. You were doing well until that tall chap with the Scottie dog tripped you up," he added helpfully.

"Be that as it may. To be dragged around the ring like an extra from *Ben Hur* by a hulking Great Dane on heat is not my idea of an undercover operation. This will be noted in my report."

"Sorry sir," replied Monro, privately thinking 'It serves you right for nicking the big dogs and leaving me with oversize cats.'

Fraser had managed to avoid dog duty altogether, and had decided to make himself scarce. Instead he wandered around the main ring chatting to various people, among which were his good friends Duncan MacPherson and Sergeant Gordon. Carefully avoiding Cumberland, Fraser was eventually buttonholed by Monro.

"Well, have you discovered anything useful?" enquired the DI.

"Oh yes, Sir. I think that I have made a breakthrough, sir."

"And…"

"A reliable source has told me of the existence of the transmitters, two of which must be activated at the same time to signal the start of a full-scale rebellion."

Monro was elated and excited; and to think that he had thought that Fraser had been obstructive from the start. "Excellent, Sergeant. And we can nip the Rebellion in the bud before it starts."

"And I know where all three are, sir. They are all held by the leaders of the rebellion."

"Fraser, you're a star. Go on."

"One is held by Charles Stuart himself."

"Of course and…?"

"One is held by the Organiser of the Rebellion."

"Ah Mr Macbig, that makes sense, and the third?"

"In the possession of a dog, sir."

"A dog?"

"Yes, sir. Swallowed, sir."

"Are you saying that one of the leaders of the Rebellion is a dog?"

"No sir, I am saying that when I attempted to arrest a suspicious-looking character, he arranged for his transmitter to be swallowed by a dog, sir."

"Would you recognize him again?"

"Difficult to say sir, but the tail was distinctive."

"I meant the Rebel, you idiot!"

"Sorry sir! It was so quick that I think that he was in disguise, sir."

"What makes you think he was in disguise?"

"We don't get many Astronauts in these parts, anyway not since the failed Findhorn – Kinloss mission to Mars. I am fairly sure that he was an imposter."

"What about the dog?"

"As far as I can recall, the dog was not disguised as an Astronaut."

"So you would probably recognise it?"

"I could have a go, sir."

There was nothing for it, thought Monro. This was too good an opportunity to miss, and he decided that an identity parade should be held as quickly as possible. A collection of possible suspects were soon marching down the high street to the police station, guarded by uniformed officers in a canine 'Perps' walk. Flora and I, and a crowd of others ,watched in amazement as the procession marched past. The dogs looked despondent as they all knew that they were guilty of something, the little stain on the best carpet, the half-chewed slipper hidden beneath the settee. The sheepdog looked sheepish, the bloodhound looked depressed.

Oscar the Red Labrador was confused. He could see that he was in trouble but had no idea why. He had run round the ring like they wanted and would have run a lot faster if there had not been a heavy weight on the end of his lead. Oscar generally woke up confused and usually became more puzzled as the day wore on until it was time for bed. The humans looked angry he thought. Perhaps I'll do my sorrowful bit with droopy eyes, head between my paws and hope that they would not notice him.

"Take your time, Sergeant. Can you see the dog that swallowed the bug?"

Fraser scratched the stubble on his chin and looked thoughtful. "It was so quick," he observed. "And not being a dog lover they all look alike to me."

"Well what sort of size was it?"

"It was a long way away. Perhaps if they all turned sideways."

"Gentleman and Ladies, please could you turn to the left." Remarkably Monro's command was carried out by the dogs, all apart from Twiglet that is. Monro corrected this with an additional command 'Bloody Hell'.

"Perhaps if I could see more of their faces," suggested Fraser.

Monro obliged, "Would numbers 3, 8 and 11 please take their hats off."

"The one with the beard. Could it come a bit nearer."

"Will number 6 face the front and step forward."

Fraser took a step forward himself and scrutinized the Wire Terrier, shaking his head negatively as he did so. "The dog I saw had green eyes, I am sure of it."

"Would all the dogs with green eyes take one step forward please." Understandably none of the dogs moved. Monro was just about to arrange them himself when the penny dropped. How could Fraser notice the colour of the eyes but not the size or shape of the animal? He was beginning to think he was involved in a wild dog chase. Unfortunately, this was the moment that DCI Cumberland walked in.

"What the f*ck's going on?" Twiglet immediately obeyed this instruction and started chasing his tail in ever tighter circles. Cumberland's response of 'Do stop that' had no effect whatsoever. The other dogs became excited and one or two tried it themselves. Others wandered off bored and started to sniff each other's bottoms. Very soon the place was in chaos. Fraser regretted the fact that his police station was being abused with dogs scratching the desks, jumping on the chairs and urinating against the filing cabinets, but it was all in a good cause. Besides, it was the first time that the cabinets had been used for anything useful in years.

"Monro. I have never seen anything like this in all my time in the police force. Do you know how ridiculous you look, you're in danger turning us into a laughing stock. We are supposed to be not drawing attention to ourselves."

"One of them has swallowed the recording device, Gov."

"Well, just fill the dogs up with food and water and lock them up until we can see what comes out. Then, Monro, you can have the pleasure of sifting through the deposits."

"But, Gov…"

"No buts, Monro. The Dog Show is now over and we should put on our disguises for the barbecue. They had better be good, Fraser, after Monro's idiocy half the village could recognise us."

Sergeant Fraser was not entirely sure that the costumes he had managed to obtain would meet Cumberland's criteria of 'good'. He had great difficulty, over the last few days, of finding any fancy dress outfits at all for the DCI and his men. Fraser had rung 14 different shops from Inverness to Aberdeen and they had all reported a huge surge in demand for costumes in the last few weeks. A typical response came from 'Party Wear' in Nairn, a fancy dress shop specializing in Nazi Uniforms and Regalia (By appointment to the Royal Family).

"Very little left in, I'm afraid. Colonel MacPherson hired most of our stock recently."

"But what about your stock of giant pigeon costumes? The last time we met you said that they had not been on hire since the Royal *It's A Knockout* in the eighties."

"The Colonel especially wanted those."

What on earth was the Colonel up to wondered Fraser? Was he planning another *It's a Royal Knockout*? No doubt his good friend will tell him in due course. Putting his curiosity out of his mind, he continued with the matter in hand.

"Well what have you got left? Have you still got Snow White and the Seven Dwarves? That would be perfect for the people I have in mind."

"Afraid not."

"The Colonel again?"

"Oh yes," the store owner replied looking through the pages of his stock book, "I have some policeman uniforms, the Colonel didn't want those."

Cumberland had not actually said 'no police uniforms' recalled Fraser and as his men were plain clothes cops, a uniform would be some sort of disguise. Monro would probably be daft enough to understand the logic of this argument but the DCI would probably just shout at him, thought Fraser.

"I'm afraid that's not really appropriate for us either."

"I also have an Adolph Hitler and a Hermann Goering suit left. They've not been much in demand since Prince Albert joined the Navy."

Again Fraser was very tempted; he would love to see Cumberland and Monroe dressed as that particular dynamic duo. "I tell you what, I will come in tomorrow morning and select out of what stock you have left. Time is short, and I need something for tomorrow morning and select out of what stock you have left."

And so, Sergeant Fraser had collected a motley collection of outfits that morning and now began unpacking the boxes, looking expectedly at the expression on Cumberland's face as he did so. Fury was a better description than anger, but Fraser manfully defended himself against his superior with the convincing argument that there was little else to choose from. Cumberland did agree that he had no wish to portray himself as an arrogant Nazi dictator with Monro as his buffoon sidekick, and was happy with the alternatives of being half a pantomime horse, a banana or dressing up as a woman, Mother Theresa in fact, or a variety of other unsuitable characters. He settled on the last box as suitable for himself and Monro. The white shirt, bow ties and bowler hats would make them look dignified he thought, and so they should be as Fraser had escribed the costumes of the former Prime Ministers 'Anthony Asquith' and 'David Lloyd George'. Fraser carefully hid the lid of the box, which said that the costumes were actually those of 'Stan Laurel and Oliver Hardy'.

Fraser had quite enjoyed disrupting Cumberland's operation and, more importantly keeping the police away from MacPherson and his men. Of course the whole thing was a complete fiction. There were no transmitters; the Colonel had come up with the whole idea. Still he would enjoy watching DI Monro looking for one later on, amidst whatever canine excrement had materialised by then.

SATURDAY AFTERNOON

– A VERY GRAVE MATTER

The barbecue was the usual fare of burnt meat and soggy salad. The diners were required to walk down a line of volunteer chefs and choose from a range of dazzling delicacies such as black pudding, haggis and by way of light relief, sausages and chicken. Reverend Wild was in charge of the sausages and as each one was handed over there was a brief accompanying message. As Fraser made his way to the head of the queue he could make out the words 'May the Lord bless this sausage and protect the consumer thereof.' Finally the Sergeant's turn arrived.

"Hello Sergeant, sausage? O Lord, bless this sausage and protect Sergeant Fraser, the consumer thereof. And if you, O Lord, could protect the rest of the sausages from scorching while I search out some more bread rolls we would indeed be doubly blessed."

The Reverend had not been the same since he discovered God. This coincided with his trip to see the Convenor of The Church of Scotland, a few weeks earlier. He had been summoned in haste shortly after Sergeant Fraser had delivered the report required from him by the Religious Crimes Act. This was one report that Fraser could not get out of, and it had caused him considerable anguish. For an hour and a half he had struggled with the questions, even sharpening the pencils did not seem to help. It also did not help that Fraser had not actually been to Church for some time. *When was that*, he thought casting his mind back, *ah yes – it was his christening*. He assumed that nothing much had changed in the last 50 years. After a few attempts to fill in the form from his virtually non-existent memories Fraser thought that there was nothing for it – he might actually have to go to Church on Sunday. Faced with this appalling prospect he finally decided to do what many of us are driven to do – he would copy the answers from a similar form. Alas, as this was a new form, RA 2, required by the Convenor's Office, there were no earlier reports to copy from. Rummaging through his filing cabinet there were remarkably few reports of any kind to copy from. In desperation and a cold sweat he rummaged through every single folder, emptying the contents in the middle of the desk, a process that did not take very long. All of a sudden there was the solution, a shaft of sunlight highlighted his Fourth Form School Report. As this had exactly the same number of boxes, all he had to do was match the answers up as best as he could with the form RA 2 for the Convenor. Fraser silently thanked the Lord for this minor miracle and settled down to work, pencil in hand.

School Sports – Throws himself in enthusiastically and is never happier than when covered in mud.

That will do for question 3, thought Fraser.

French –　　　　He has come on well this year, and can make himself understood in simple sentences.

I'll put that one in Box 1, he decided.

Latin –　　　　He lacks interest in the subject and feels that it has no relevance to modern life, especially as all those involved are long since dead.

Science –　　　Rarely contributes, and is often found sitting at the back with the other troublemakers.

They will do for 2 and 4, only two more to go. Fraser was beginning to feel pleased with himself. It was a shame that his school report had not been particularly good, but then neither was it particularly bad so the Form RA 2 would probably be quite convincing.

Domestic Science – A disaster – only prompt action by the fire brigade prevented his experiment with bread from burning the place down.

Box 7 seem relevant for that one.

English & Drama – Has made a significant improvement in dramatics and his death scenes are a joy to behold.

That can go in Box 6, thought Fraser, leaving the last one to go in Box 5.

Class Behaviour – Gets on well generally, but like many of
　　　　　　　　his age, is often distracted from his work by
　　　　　　　　members of the opposite sex.

Fraser leaned back in his chair with a sense of satisfaction. He would just have time to put this in the letter box and catch the last post after which he deserved a rewarding pint at the Crown and Usurper. It was several days later that the Convenor received the following report:

RELIGIOUS CRIMES ACT 2007 FORM RA 2		
REPORT TO THE CONVENOR ON	CHURCH: FINDHORN CLERGY: REV. D. WILD REPORT BY: SERGEANT FRASER	
1	COMMUNICATION SKILLS	HE HAS COME ON WELL THIS YEAR AND CAN MAKE HIMSELF UNDERSTOOD IN SIMPLE SENTENCES
2	KNOWLEDGE OF THE BIBLE	HE LACKS INTEREST IN THE SUBJECT AND FEELS THAT IT HAS NO RELEVANCE TO MODERN LIFE, ESPECIALLY AS EVERYONE INVOLVED IS NOW DEAD
3	PERFORMANCE AT BURIALS	THROWS HIMSELF IN ENTHUSIASTICALLY AND IS NEVER HAPPIER THAN WHEN COVERED IN MUD
4	PERFORMANCE AS WEDDINGS	RARELY CONTRIBUTES AND IS USUALLY FOUND SITTING AT THE BACK WITH THE OTHER TROUBLEMAKERS
5	RELATIONSHIP WITH CONGREGATION	GETS ON WELL GENERALLY BUT LIKE MANY OF HIS AGE HE IS OFTEN DISTRACTED FROM HIS WORK BY MEMBERS OF THE OPPOSITE SEX
6	ABILITY TO DELIVER A SERMON	HE HAS MADE A SIGNIFICANT IMPROVEMENT IN DRAMATICS AND HIS DEATH SCENES ARE A JOY TO BEHOLD
7	PERFORMANCE AT COMMUNION	A DISASTER – ONLY PROMPT ACTION BY THE FIRE BRIGADE PREVENTED HIS EXPERIMENT WITH BREAD FROM BURNING THE WHOLE PLACE DOWN
THIS REPORT IS CONFIDENTIAL AND SHOULD NOT BE SHOWN TO THE SUBJECT		

It should come as no surprise to note that the Church considered this report to be a very grave matter indeed.

The Church of Scotland was fairly egalitarian in nature. The Moderator, elected by the clergy to hold office for one year at a time, was the official head of the church but the real day-to-day power lay with the Secretariat, headed by the Convenor. Again this was an elective post, theoretically held for two years at a time, ensuring some continuity by overlapping with the annual Moderators. In practice, the Right Reverend Rabbie Kray had held the post for the last 18 years. The post was up again for election the following month and the smart money was on Rabbie Kray to be re-elected once more. As there were no other candidates, this did seem the most likely result. In the early days there had been opposition candidates but they would almost always withdraw their candidacy at the last moment, invariably to carry out missionary work in Africa, or wherever else the Reverend Kray suggested might be good for their continued health. A tall, thin man the Reverend Kray was always immaculately dressed, usually in Designer labelled clothes such as 'Clergy by Gucci' or 'For Ever and Ever, Armani'. He could be very charming when he needed something, but otherwise he would be dogmatic and unresponsive. He did not tolerate fools gladly; in fact he did not tolerate anyone gladly and was best avoided. The Reverend took very seriously his role in ensuring appropriate behaviour within the Church, and under his 'guidance' there were few of those scandals that dogged its sister Church over the border in England. All potential issues were identified at an early stage and the problems buried immediately without trace, as occasionally were the clergy responsible.

To help him maintain discipline in the Church, the Convenor had established Unit 19 run by the Reverends Spinks and Perkins, known as Pinky and Perky behind their backs but never, ever, to their face. Unit 19 was a sort of 'Scottish Inquisition' but obviously without the fun bits associated with the Spanish original. Spinks and Perkins had established a fearsome reputation, and to merely receive an invitation to discuss ecumenical matters at their office, the notorious Room 19 situated in the basement of St Faith's Church, had been enough to make some clergy leave the country for missionary work in Madrassahs on Pakistan's North West frontier, this being considered the safer option.

When the Reverend Wild received such an invitation he was concerned, but also puzzled. He was not aware of any issues that would have attracted the attention of Unit 19. There was the matter with the Organist and her various organs, but surely no one knew about that. He arrived apprehensively at Room 19, a featureless and windowless basement box. The back of the door was covered with insulating material and the whole room was obviously designed to be sound proof. The Reverend Kray was prone to joke that 'In St Faith's, no one can hear you scream.'

The interview went surprisingly well, thought the Reverend Wild. The heavy antique James VI Bible with the jewel-encrusted wooden cover was accidentally dropped on his fingers a few times during the reading of uplifting passages from the Bible, but the Reverend Perkins was quick to apologise on each of the 17 occasions. And the Reverend Spinks was genuinely mortified to think that he nearly drowned a member of the clergy by pouring several bottles of communal wine down said clergyman's throat; the muslin cloth used to filter out the sediment being a particular problem as it stuck in the throat, causing Wild great difficulty in breathing. Still, it was nice of Spinks to have offered him a drink in the first place, to break the ice as Spinks put it.

Some of the Bible readings were new to Wild. He did not recall the passages 'Thou shalt not be distracted by female members of the congregation' and 'If thy findeth thyself in a hole, thou should stop digging and report the matter to thy Lord.'

He also found the questions put to him by the Reverend Kray very strange.

"Tell me about your obsession with premature burial?"

"Have you read a lot of Edgar Allan Poe recently?"

"Can you demonstrate a dying scene for us?"

The strangest discussion of all revolved around the revelation that everyone in the Bible was dead.

The Reverend Wild pointed out that:

1) Jesus was not dead, and
2) What was death anyway but a gateway to immortality in the presence of the Lord.

Kray was most impressed by these arguments, and surprised that a member of the Clergy believed in God. Perhaps there was something in this religion stuff after all. He would have to read the book.

The conversation turned to the inhabitants of Findhorn Parish and whether there were any peculiarities or suspicious behaviour. That took up the rest of the afternoon and the early evening. Finally it was agreed that the Convenor would make a surprise visit to the International Dog Show and Ceilidh, where Wild would point out any suspicious villagers or locals who might fall under the categories of sinners, blasphemers, and people who watched *Footballers Wives*, a sort of catch-all category. Satisfied, the Reverend Kray allowed Wild to leave with handshakes and smiles all round, which was a painful experience for Wild due to the earlier accidents.

***

Cumberland was puzzled. As far as he could tell the only ones that appeared to be in fancy dress were policemen. Fraser had not bothered to mention that the fancy dress was to be judged in the evening before the start of the Ceilidh, or that it was a competition for children only. Nevertheless his men were in disguise and this seemed to be working. The police in a variety of costumes had shadowed likely suspects but nothing of substance had been picked up so far; there had been little sign of overt terrorist activity. Nevertheless the members of the 'Rabbie Burns Unit' were determined to track down the remaining transmitters and, once again, I was checked by Hawkins and his dog, managing to pass muster by putting on an unconvincing false Scottish accent. Hawkins thought that I must have recently been released back into the community, whereas the dog thought that

I was weird and best avoided. The Colonel, who was personally being monitored by DI Monro, took great delight in mischievously approaching complete strangers and, within the earshot of Monro, stating that ,The Eagle Has Landed' or 'It's on for Tuesday night' although the latter phrase when delivered with a wink caused a certain amount of confusion with one gentleman, who went so far as booking a hotel room for himself and the Colonel.

Cumberland had kept himself aloof, and left the detailed observation to the others. As a result he was the first to notice a sudden commotion coming from the direction of the food stalls. He could make out Sergeant Fraser being chased by someone disguised as a Vicar. Clever these terrorists, thought the DCI, who would have suspected a man of the cloth? But clearly Fraser had rumbled him and needed support.

A quick call to Monro and the Pursuit was organised. Cumberland, being the nearest, was the first into the churchyard, hot on the heels of Murray and Fraser, catching up with them by the freshly dug grave of Jim Grundy which was awaiting its future occupant. The Council had helpfully provided a fire extinguisher on a stand as an emergency precaution against spontaneous combustion. By the time that Cumberland arrived, Fraser and Murray were teetering on the edge of the grave locked in hand-to-hand struggle, rather like the famous drawing of Sherlock Holmes and Moriarty grappling at the Reichanbach Falls. Fraser had managed to force Murray into dropping the poker but the Reverend soon discovered the fire extinguisher as a suitable alternative weapon, and very effective it was as Cumberland found out to his cost. Swinging the extinguisher round in a circle the Reverend had just missed contact with the side of Fraser's head, due to the quick evasive action taken by the Sergeant. Unfortunately Cumberland took no such action and there was a definite thud as metal met skin and bone. Stunned, Cumberland slowly tumbled back into the open grave, his bowler hat gliding gracefully in after him.

Sergeant Fraser and the Reverend Murray concluded a momentary armistice as the likely consequences of sending a Detective Chief Constable to an early grave sank in.

Fraser noticed a fleet of vehicles pulling up outside the churchyard. He recognised the first car, a Mercedes with tinted windows, not only from the distinctive number plate CON 1, but also from the silver cross that had replaced the Mercedes emblem on the bonnet. The Convenor's vehicle was quickly followed by two people movers from the Church Of Scotland IncidenT Support Unit, identified by the distinctive slogan 'COS ITS U'. The vans had soon emptied their cargo of burly-looking clergymen, obviously spoiling for a fight. There was a motto in Unit 19, 'we practise what others preach'. The convoy was completed by another Mercedes, CON 2, making up the rearguard with Spinks and Perkins inside. The Reverend Rabbie Kray had decided to take no chances and had come mob-handed.

As the clergy grouped for a spiritual briefing outside the churchyard, Fraser and the Reverend Wild simultaneously, and independently of each other, thanked the Lord for deliverance. Wild had no idea who he would 'finger' in the words of Rabbie Kray. He had prayed every night that week for a solution to his predicament and then, heaven sent, appeared a bunch of English policemen hell-bent on causing trouble. The Reverend Wild greeted the visiting clergy with an impromptu speech that was soon cut short.

"We're not here for small talk, Wild," said Reverend Kray abruptly, "Where are these deviants? They had better exist or there will be trouble."

"Oh, they definitely exist, your worship, can't you see? They are the ones dressed in strange pagan costumes."

Kray took off his dark glasses and surveyed the scene, noticing Constable and Sargent walking past in their equine outfit.

"Good Heavens," said the Reverend Convenor, "you are right, Findhorn does seem to be a very strange place indeed. There appears to be a primitive form of horse worship."

The Reverend was further shocked when PC Harris walked by dressed as a banana. "And a fertility cult!" he exclaimed, "We have not arrived a moment too soon, just look at what's going on," he exclaimed as various Police Officers wandered by in fancy dress.

While this had been going on, Sergeant Fraser had been telling Monro the good news. "DC Monro, can I have a word?"

"What about? I shouldn't be seen talking to you, it will blow my cover."

"I'm not sure that it will do that," observed Fraser cynically, "but you asked me to keep an eye open for anything out of the ordinary."

"Yes, well get on with it!"

"I think that I have noticed something. Those men at

152

the gate, pretending to be clergymen, I think that they are the ones I saw on the High Moor," lied Fraser.

"I see what you mean, thank you Sergeant. I will make sure that DCI Cumberland will hear about your responsibility for this news. Have you seen the DCI by the way?"

"He saw him earlier; he must be around somewhere, perhaps having a quiet nap."

"That leaves me in charge, good," beamed Monro. "Now perhaps we can get on with some proper Police work. Calling all units, this is DC Monro. We have located suspected terrorists at the front of the Church, by the lych gate. Prepare for arrest position and make sure that you do not make a move until I give the word."

The clergy moved purposefully into the churchyard crossing themselves as they moved into this den of sin. The Police pretended not to notice them as both sides warily circled each other, neither wanting to make the first move and lose the element of surprise. It was a struggle that had been going on for hundreds of years – Church versus State. Of course, neither side realised this.

Attracted by the site of the freshly dug grave, the Reverend Kray looked down into the trench before summoning over his two lieutenants for a second opinion.

Cumberland had been badly stunned by his fall. Hearing voices he was able to raise an eyelid to see a group of clergy silhouetted in the sunlight discussing his condition.

Gazing down at the motionless body of DCI Cumberland, Perkins was in no doubt. The Stan Laurel costume and Cumberland's natural pallor were entirely convincing, "He looks dead to me, no problem."

Spinks took a look for himself. He had never seen a better-prepared corpse; a deathly white face, a proper old-fashioned burial suit all topped off with a bowler hat. "No doubt at all, he's genuine, not one of Wild's weirdos," he concluded.

I'm not dead, just a bit dazed thought Cumberland gingerly moving his right arm to see if it was broken. Perkins broke into a cold sweat as the cadaver slowly raised an accusing right hand, pointing at him with a spindly digit.

"Why me?" he exclaimed.

"Jesus!" said Spinks.

"Lazarus, more like," responded Kray, now thoroughly alarmed. He had seen nothing like it in his entire career. This was worse than he thought. Perhaps Wild had sold his soul to the devil, or vampirism had taken root in Findhorn which was the more likely given the reputation of the place.

Cumberland slowly raised himself to his feet, his eyes still glazed from the bang to the back of his head. The ecclesiastical trio backed off before this apparition only to bump into Batman and Robin, soon to be joined by Oliver Hardy.

"Holy…" Perkins started to say before he was interrupted.

"I'm arresting you under the Prevention of Terrorism Act."

Cumberland unaware of what was going on and anxious to obtain confirmation of his present status tapped Kray on the shoulder who turned round to face his pasty-faced tormentor. "I'm not dead," he maintained. This was enough for Kray who broke and ran. Perkins and Spinks were made of sterner stuff and stood their ground.

"Follow him," shouted Monro to Sargent and Constable. The pantomime horse shook its head – more of a nay than a neigh. "Just get after him, he looks like the ringleader."

Sargent and Constable did their best. In fact they did very well trotting after Kray, tackling most obstacles with aplomb. They vaulted the open grave in perfect unison in a sequence that would have graced the Horse of the Year Show. In fact if they had not responded to the round of applause by performing the standard pantomime horse bow with four crossed legs, they may well have caught the Convenor before he reached his Mercedes.

A general melee had broken out in the Church grounds as the Police Force attempted to arrest the Terrorists and the Clergy tried to detain the Terrorists, and the Clergy tried to detain the deviants. The clamour attracted from the crowd and a steady stream of people began to line the Church walls, puzzled at what was going on. Colonel MacPherson and myself were among the first to observe the skirmish. There was a wry smile on the Colonel's face as he watched the proceedings unfold, and did his best to offer shouts of encouragement to the Police, such as 'Lovely Left Hook, Mother Theresa' and 'Watch your back Hitler'. The most common of all, and which the rest of the crowd soon took up, were warnings to Sargent and Constable of 'Behind You' creating the atmosphere of a matinee performance at a Christmas Panto. I suppose that I also looked on with a sense of amusement, but also relief that the attention of the 'Burns' unit had been diverted elsewhere.

It was certainly a sight to behold. Mother Theresa was holding her own against Reverends Billy and Charlie, who had been a professional tag wrestling team in former careers. Billy was pounding the earth as a sign of submission, while Charlie grabbed Mother Theresa's hair in an attempt to pull her off his colleague. Inevitably the wig came off causing Charlie to fall over backwards, hitting his head on a tombstone. There was a brief look of surprise on Charlie's face before he passed out completely. The text on the tombstone was 'I submit to thee, O Lord, thy wonders to behold.' Mother Theresa was soon to be seen standing over the prone figure of Charlie with a triumphal fist in the air – the winner, by one fall and a submission.

PC Harris had great difficulty moving about with his weighty banana skin and it was not long before he had fallen over, unable to get up again unaided. Almost inevitably, a number of other Policemen tripped on him during the course of the skirmish, together with a number of Kray's men. Thanks to Harris and Mother Theresa, the clergy from Unit 19 were already wavering when PCs Hitler and Goering launched a blitzkreig attack from the flank. Kray's men quickly turned and fled to their waiting vehicles, pursued by the jubilant police force and within minutes the churchyard had emptied. Both sides piled into their respective vehicles as, with the smell of burning rubber and the sound of screeching engines, they all headed off in the direction of Inverness.

Fraser was the last person to leave the churchyard as he gave a fireman's lift to Cumberland who had once more passed out, worn out by obtaining a second opinion on his state of health. Fraser had decided that this was an opportune moment to curry favour with the DCI, as well as a good time to put a bit of distance between himself and the Reverend Murray.

Very soon, it was as if nothing had happened. The Churchyard was empty again, save for the prone figure of the Reverend Charlie.

The Colonel was laughing his head off at this unexpected turn of events, joined by Sergeant Gordon and several of his men.

"I don't think that we will be seeing anymore of Special Branch today," MacPherson prophesised correctly. "Perhaps we can now enjoy the Ceilidh without interruption."

SATURDAY NIGHT –

THE ROYAL VISIT

The Ceilidh was an anticlimax after the rest of the day's events. The police had scattered all over the High Moor looking for The Reverend Kray and the rest of his terrorist gang, and so didn't bother to put in an appearance. A bit of a disappointment, really, all things considered. The Findhorn Swingers carried out their annual 'Glen Miller Massacre', as the Colonel called it. The Colonel himself didn't sink to the bottom of the Firth, living to Pipe another day, and the 'Norse Dancers' only had one serious casualty this year, and even he was expected to live according to the Doctors.

The highlight of the evening, if you did not count Snoop Dougy Dougal, a lively 14-year-old rap artist articulating the vibrant urban street culture of Findhorn (non-school nights only), was Lady MacPherson. She actually played quite beautifully and sang even more beautifully, which was quite an achievement considering the piano badly needed tuning. I had never come across anyone with such a complete musical ear, that every duff note on the piano was echoed by a compensating adjustment to the composer's vocal score. The maniacal effect was at once quite amazing, and very, very scary. One of the songs struck a chord, or would have done but for the fact that a chord was a sequence of notes in a pre-arranged order. It would be more accurate to say that I recognised one of the pieces as the fourth of Richard Strauss's 'Four Last Songs,' written towards the end of the composer's life and suffused by his melancholy preoccupation with death. I am sure that hearing Lady Ann's version would have encouraged Strauss to hasten his own inevitable end.

Flora looked a delight in her white dress adorned only with a single tartan sash. She was the life and soul of the dance floor, her auburn locks reflecting her body movements, waving this way and that in time to the music. For my part I was not so co-ordinated, and excused myself after the first dance to avoid further embarrassment. Flora assured me that in between dances, younger residents should take part in 'The Ceremony Tossing The Caber' in the committee rooms by the side of the village hall. It was part of the village tradition she insisted and besides, she needed to find out whether everything under the kilt was in perfect working order. Unfortunately, all the rooms were in use by the Swingers, who were busy filling up every nook and cranny with their instruments. And so, almost inevitably, I was to be frustrated once more.

Nevertheless, I am surprised to say that I actually enjoyed the evening. The whole village seemed to take part in one way or another even if it was only to apply bandages, and there was a real sense of community, the sense of community that often arose in out of the way Scottish villages. I had the overwhelming feeling that they were all slightly unhinged and that because of this uniformity, everything seemed quite normal; nothing seemed out of place. I suppose that it was this slight madness that encouraged the earlier Jacobites to charge lines of well-drilled Redcoats, running into well-aimed volleys of musket fire armed only with the 18th Century equivalent of a dustbin lid and a machete. You had to like these people.

We arrived back at Castle Brady at about 11pm, and I was immediately invited into the Colonel's study for the inevitable 'wee dram'.

"That went very well," the Colonel declared with a satisfied look on his face.

"How so?" I enquired.

"The day has been a great success," MacPherson insisted.

"But surely the presence of Special Branch hindered the meetings that you had planned?"

"We had no real need to meet up. The main planning was completed long ago. I met the lads early this morning for a final briefing well before the Dog Show started and they then returned to their units. After that we just needed to distract Special Branch's attention while the rebellion commenced. Mind you The Reverend Kray and his Clergy turning up was a real godsend, quite literally," he chuckled. "Cumberland must have spent hours chasing them round the moor this evening."

"Has the rebellion started in London? Has Charles Stuart already landed?" I enquired with genuine interest.

"No, laddie. The rebellion has commenced here, where it should, just a few miles from where the last one ended." He cocked his head to listen attentively, as we both detected the sound of vehicles pulling up on the gravel outside of the front entrance, followed by muffled sounds of shouted instructions.

"They have arrived. I think that you should come and greet our guests, laddie. While we were at the Ceilidh, the boys carried out a commando-style raid on Balmoral. We have just decapitated the government, in a manner of speaking. We have kidnapped the Queen and the Prime Minister, the two Heads of State, and they will both be joining us very shortly."

"But what about the Police, the Guards, and the Army?"

"I told you that we have a lot of supporters, especially in this part of the country. We have been planning this for years. It was always been the Achilles heel of the monarchy that they venture into the Scottish heartland every year, wandering round Balmoral dressed in kilts and pretending to care about the Scottish people. Imagine! We have to put up with a so-called Prince of Wales wearing a sporran. Well no more, I am pleased to say that the raid went like clockwork. Mind you, we had not thought of black pudding to distract the Corgis, I will give you all the credit for that."

I followed the Colonel into the hall and joined the others assembling in a line by the front door, resembling the presentation line for a film premiere.

Sergeant Gordon appeared, full of the enthusiasm that is generated by a job well done. "It all went like clockwork

161

Sir, even the black pudding worked a treat…" He fell silent seeing the look of thunder on Mrs McGregor's face.

"Excellent Gordon, well done. Bring our guests through will you, there's a good chap, it wouldn't do to keep them waiting. And get the men ready for tomorrow. Pass on my appreciation to the lads and an extra dram all round."

"Thank you, Colonel." The Sergeant saluted and retired to do as he was bidden.

We were alone together for a few minutes, the Major, Brendan, Erik, Mrs McGregor, and myself, fidgeting as you do while standing and waiting. I passed a few moments deciding on a suitable film title for our pseudo film premiere line-up. Based on the Sergeant's remarks 'A Clockwork Black Pudding' was the first film to spring to mind. Rapidly passing over 'The Castle Brady Bunch' and 'Whisky Galore', and deciding that 'Braveheart' was too obvious, I settled on another film starring Mal Gibbon – 'Mad Mac's 2'. This musing was eventually brought to an end by the arrival of 'our guests' at the front door, escorted by Sergeant Gordon.

The Prime Minister was the first to enter and strode purposefully into the room. Instantly latching on to the Colonel as the person in charge he shook MacPherson's hand vigorously.

"Ah, Colonel. Heard about this plan of yours. Look… I think that we can sort this out. I mean… I am a supporter of the Scottish. I wasn't always, but I became interested in Scottishness at University… became pretty convinced that Scottishness was the way forward. I have done a lot for the Scottish people… I have protected their ancient ways and culture… ill health, dependence on the state, the right to have three fishing boats for every fish in the North Sea… that sort of thing. You can trust me on this one. The Queen… ghastly woman… have to make polite conversation to her once a week. Horrible… family worse, always on the make. Time to get rid of the lot.

"I think that we could do a deal. Tell you what… um… just thinking aloud here… perhaps it would be easiest if… I know… I could replace the Queen to start with. I would get a lot of support on this one, trust me. I would tell it to the people straight. I could say that the Queen was just about to mount a coup. No, it has to be more serious than that. Ah yes, got it, mounting a coup and joining the Euro. We could throw in some stuff about recruiting for the police solely from the Polish community. That should turn the people against her. I am sure that the 'spooks' could produce some documents, downloads, that sort of thing. Can be pretty convincing, I can tell you. So, again just coming out with some ideas here… so I could do the first slot, take all the flak, that sort of thing. Say first 5 years, perhaps a bit longer if necessary. Your man could be the royal consort. No, the wife would kill me. She has always wanted to wear tiaras. Keeps several in her drawer just in case. How about 'Deputy King' or… or 'Prince'. What's your chap's name? Perfect, he could be Prince Charles, next in line to the throne. You know, there is a bit of a resemblance. The Archbishop of Canterbury might be a bit tricky on this, but no matter. I could always get the Pope to crown me. Personal friend you know. Ah… I see it's time to go to my room, freshen up etc. I will work on the details and perhaps we could catch up later. Ciao."

The Colonel stood open-mouthed, impressed by this bravura performance. There could be a role for him in the new government, Minister of Information perhaps.

The Queen appeared in the front door and proceeded down the corridor. Glad to see the back of the Prime Minister disappearing up the stairs, she switched into full royal mode.

"Hello and what do you do?"

"I'm the housekeeper Ma'am," replied Mrs McGregor.

"Ah, the woman in charge."

Mrs McGregor blushed and warmed to the Queen at once. It was strange how often women liked or hated each other on the first encounter. The Queen put Mrs McGregor at ease straight away with her practised manner, homing on the little things that were important to the individuals she was in conversation with at the time. Despite her fundamental belief in the Jacobite cause, Mrs McGregor had always admired the Queen and having met her face to face she thought that in other circumstances they could have been the best of friends. The result was a lively discussion on the best way to remove grass stains from jodhpurs, and which only came to an inconclusive end when Colonel McPherson intervened, hastening the Queen further down the line to meet Brendan. My heart started thumping when I realised the subject that these two most had in common was probably grouse shooting and wellingtons, and I doubt that the latter would naturally come up in conversation. Fearing a major incident, I was relieved that Brendan, awestruck merely by being in the same room as HRH, mumbled something unintelligible about the weather, which the Queen acknowledged with a nod before moving on to Erik.

"Hello and what is your job?"

"I am man in charge of zecurity," replied Erik.

"We have one of those. He's not very good. One takes security very seriously these days. One has to stop one's husband getting out at night, and of course to stop people getting in," she said looking pointedly at Sergeant Gordon who had followed her through the front door. Turning back to Erik she instructed, "You must come and see me."

"And what do you do?" she said, stopping in front of me.

"At the moment, I am a pretend young Pretender, your Majesty."

"That sounds an interesting job. Does it take much time? How do you pretend? How often do you pretend? Are you pretending now?

"Can't you tell?"

"Oh, yes. Now I can see," she frowned slightly as she asked the next question. "Is there any point to being a Pretender?"

"I'm not just about there being a point, I am a point. A focal point."

"Oh, sounds a bit like being Queen." Finally, she moved on to the Major.

"Your face is awfully familiar. Reminds one of a lady-in-waiting I once had. Lovely girl. Left with a bit of a fuss. One can't remember why, but these things usually involved one's husband."

The Major said nothing, but there was a strange glint in his eye.

SUNDAY MORNING –

CULLODEN

I was the last down to breakfast again, after another sleepless night. I had been moved to the east wing well away from Flora. I had no doubt that this was on the orders of Lady Anne. I had joined the Major, the Queen and the PM in the 'naughty annex' guarded by Erik and his staff, who took it in turns to sit in the corridor pretending to be awake. I had been given the room next to the PM, who seemed to spend the entire night rehearsing speeches. All I could make out, not that I particularly wanted to listen, was something about 'A New Dawn has broken' and this at 3 o'clock in the morning!

As a result I had slept badly, ending up dreaming of headless ghosts, or to be more accurate, I had dreamt of one headless ghost, namely myself. I suppose it was not unrelated to the thought that the penalty for kidnapping a monarch was probably still punishable by beheading with an axe. I had dreamt of Flora running through the gardens of Castle

Brady with my head underarm only to be tackled by DC Monro, my head flung out of Flora's arm with the impact. I became quite dizzy as my head rolled over and over the manicured lawn, eventually coming to a halt by a bamboo bush that I recognised from the other afternoon. Kabukazi peered out from behind the leaves, and having decided that I was not the Major, or at least the part of the Major he would recognise, shrank back into the undergrowth. I wondered what had happened to my body to which I was once rather attached. They say that a human body can continue to run round a farmyard without the head for up to one minute. But as soon as I had that thought I knew that I had made a terrible mistake. Brendan appeared in my vision, and punishment was clearly in the offing as a result of this gaffe. In his youth Brendan had appeared for the under-21 Scottish Rugby team at Murrayfield on more than one occasion, and placed my head carefully on the lawn for a penalty kick. I could see the intense concentration on his face as he prepared for the conversion, focussing alternately on the ball, i.e. my head, and on his intended target which appeared to be DCI Cumberland walking on the other side of the ornamental lake. I will never know whether he managed this as mercifully I was awoken by the smell of the sizzling bacon and toast.

The smell had saved my bacon, and I hoped that some bacon had been saved for me.

I had been promised a fresh pair of trousers today, but as nothing materialised, I had to wear my kilt down to breakfast. Entering the dining room, I could see that the Colonel was just finishing his meal. The sideboard was laden with a veritable feast; plates of bacon, fried tomatoes, beans and fried eggs.

"Is there a place for me?" I enquired suspiciously, not believing my eyes.

Mrs McGregor apologised for the lamentable state of affairs. "No there's no fish, and I'm afraid that someone has stolen all the black pudding. You'll have to make do with the bacon." The Colonel looked sheepish as the housekeeper glared at him.

"Then I'll just have to make do Mrs McGregor," I sighed. "Black pudding stolen eh, who would do such a thing?" I replied, trying to be sympathetic. "There must be a tea leaf in the house."

"Aye, there's a pot on the side."

I loaded up my plate with the hitherto delicacies and was just about to tuck in when Erik arrived at the downing room door. He was quite breathless and looked embarrassed, his scar turning a bright red.

"Excuse me Herr Colonel, but we found the Queen in her dressing gown, talking to a suit of armour in the Long Hall."

I could imagine the scene. 'Hello and what do you do? Is it interesting being a suit of armour? Some of one's predecessors were suits of armour, there are pictures of them on the walls of the Palace.'

"And the Queen's clothes?" enquired the Colonel, fearing the worst.

"Gone, and so is the Major."

"What about the Prime Minister?"

"He's still with us, practising his speech in the mirror

with a chamber-pot on his head a drain plunger in one hand and a blanket over his shoulders. I am very sorry Herr Colonel; one of my men must have fallen asleep on duty. I shall of course tender my resignation immediately."

If there was still a Russian Front, I have no doubt that Erik would have sent himself there immediately, and without any supper!

Sergeant Gordon arrived in a similarly breathless state. "We've found him. He was picked up by one of the police patrols that were out looking for the Reverend Kay."

"Well we still have the Heads of State, but we must retrieve the Major; he has seen too much. Round up the lads if you would Erik. Forget about that nonsense of resigning and get the Land Rover's outside as quickly as you can, there's a good chap."

"Of course, Herr Colonel," and, with the usual round of heel clicking, Erik was off, followed quickly by Sergeant Gordon.

"Come on Charles, there is no time to lose," exclaimed MacPherson, mopping up the last bits of sauce on his plate with a piece of toast.

I, on the other hand was just about to try my first mouthful of bacon when Mrs McGregor whisked the plate away.

"Away with you and do your duty. If you're still hungry there's some bannock cake on the side that you can take with you."

Still hungry! I hadn't had a single bite to eat. Munro had spoiled my breakfast – my bacon and egg breakfast! My dislike of this policeman was growing daily. I was left with no choice except to take a couple of rock-hard bannock cakes with me, as I followed the Colonel. Already in fatigues, the Colonel paused only to put on his tam-o'-shanter, carefully checking that it was at the correct angle, before making his way outside. There we found a hive of activity as the Land Rovers were brought round, quickly filling up with 'the lads' who looked as keen as mustard for action. I managed to find a space in the Colonel's vehicle, driven by Erik, and crammed myself in the back with three others. Gordon tapped on the side window, which was promptly wound down to receive the report.

"We've tracked him down, sir. They're holding him at the new Culloden Visitors' Centre. We can be there within 15 minutes."

"Very good. Lead the way then Sergeant."

The convoy rolled through the gates of Brady Castle and down the road towards Culloden. There was an air of excitement in the vehicle as if this was the start of the long awaited Jacobite Rebellion, which in a way it was. But as the last one ended at Culloden, it could be a very short-lived rebellion indeed.

Despite his extremely sore head, Cumberland was pleased with events. They had not yet cornered the terrorist Rabby Kray, but after a wild goose chase in the Highlands of Scotland, had rounded up quite a few of his men. They had also taken into custody 'The Jacobite Conspiracy' arrested that morning on the High Moor. He was convinced that, very soon, Charles Stuart would also be in their hands. He was not too sure about his latest detainee. A batty old woman insisting that she was a person of great importance and should be released straight away, but chose to say nothing. *There might be a knighthood in it for me*, thought Cumberland. *Perhaps I could name it after this place*, he mused, 'Cumberland of Culloden'. It had a nice ring to it, evocative.

Monro was less happy. The DCI had insisted that the suspect dogs be brought with them for a third inspection and were now in the waiting van guarded by PC Maclean. Even Monro was beginning to doubt that they would find a transmitter. After the dog show fiasco, he was beginning to fear that the only fast track he would see in the future was at a greyhound race.

Alerted by the sound of a convoy pulling off the road, the police filed out of the Visitor Centre to see what was happening. Cumberland, still suffering from slight concussion and double vision, squinted through the early morning mist that still drifted over the moor, and was the first to speak.

"Is that the Army?"

"I think that you will find that it's the Jacobites," advised Fraser recognising Sergeant Gordon in the front vehicle.

Cumberland, still nursing a headache, managed a smile. A thin smile that at the same time portrayed grim determination and menace. "Well the cat has come to the canary. We will soon apprehend the lot of them and put an end to this farce," he declared.

Cumberland was determined to show leadership and instil confidence in his men by making an inspirational 'eve of battle' speech. "Now, I don't want you to let any of these men get away. They may be armed and dangerous but this is a matter of national importance. You have your weapons and do not be afraid to use them. DI Monro will take full responsibility if any of you are killed or injured."

Munro was even less impressed as, in his view, Cumberland ponced around like a latter day Wellington. He was beginning to think that the blow on the head had seriously unhinged the DCI.

"Detective Inspector, please form a Police Line, and expect riot conditions."

"Do you have a plan, sir?" enquired Monro.

"Why, to arrest those scoundrels."

It was hardly the stuff of Laurence Olivier on the eve of Agincourt, but the DI arranged the men into a main rank, with snatch squads on either flank.

Our small group of Scots observed these preliminary manoeuvres with a range of emotions. Erik looked bloodthirsty, Sergeant Gordon looked concerned as he studied the tactical problem, and of course I was seriously alarmed. Colonel MacPherson was none of these. I had not seen him so happy since he tripped up Cumberland at the dog show. His face positively shone with pleasure.

"I think that they mean business, Colonel," noted Gordon.

"I can see that, Sergeant, there is nothing for it but cold steel."

He strode purposefully to his Land Rover, took out a bag of golf clubs and returned to our group. As he issued out the irons he made morale-boosting statements such as 'They may have mace gas and marksmen but we have the hearts of Highlanders.'

My particular favourite, with hindsight was 'Remember, if you die here today you blood will mingle like that of your glorious ancestors.'

"It is time for revenge. They will not stand against a Highland charge," declared the Colonel. I think that he was becoming quite mad.

The police advanced slowly and carefully, making sure that there were no gaps in the line. After a few paces, Monro dutifully read out the 'Riot Act' warning through a loudhailer and the stage was set for the second battle of Culloden.

Cumberland was puzzled by the response of MacPherson's men. "What's going on?" he asked no one in particular.

"I think that they are preparing for a round of golf, sir," said Fraser with just a hint of sarcasm.

"But the golf balls are targeted at us," exclaimed Monro.

"They have no chance of hitting us at this range," opined Cumberland, maintaining a stiff upper lip approach. It was unfortunate that the two pieces of plaster on his forehead provided a perfect 'x marks the spot' target and almost before he had finished the word 'range', he had succumbed to another blow to the head and was lying prone at the feet of the assembled police force; just lying there, showing leadership and instilling confidence.

On the other side of the field, Colonel MacPherson was beginning to enjoy living the dream. "Always go for the officers first," he chuckled. "Soften them up with a bit of volley fire – that's where we went wrong last time."

The rest of us joined in with various degrees of accuracy. The Colonel walked behind, giving us encouragement.

"Watch that swing Gordon. Not like that Charles; here let me. Follow through with the club like this."

"Bloody hell!" shouted an injured Monro, clutching has arm. A number of other Policemen were also hit by a volley of golf balls being fired from the Jacobite ranks. Their colleagues were already escorting some to the rear. The DI resorted to the loudhailer again.

"Look, we're not larking about. You're outnumbered and we're armed. We are not going to swallow any more of your nonsense. We've well and truly cooked your goose, so be sensible and surrender."

These last remarks were too much for Brendan; with a roar he started his 400-yard run towards the Police shouting, "You Bird Baiting Bastards."

Sensing the moment the Colonel shouted, "Now lads. They're wavering," and with a roar charged forward, brandishing his number 9 iron as though his life depended on it, as well it might. Sergeant Gordon had retrieved his Pipes from the car and was playing 'MacPherson's Lament' for all he was worth. The hideous racket drove us even faster away from the skirling and towards the police. Carried away by the excitement and enthusiasm of MacPherson, and by the sheer enmity of Brendan, the 'lads' buoyed themselves up with a mixture of ancient Scottish oaths, a mixture of some Gaelic shouts that I did not understand, and plain old-fashioned war cries.

"For Scotland."

"For Charles, the rightful King."

"For Bonnie Prince Charles and Scotland."

"Banzai!"

We all pulled up short in surprise at this last one, with Kabukazi stopping in conformity. We all stared at him, and he at us. The Japanese Corporal had reasoned that whenever the Land Rovers had gone out in force they invariably came back with the Major on board. He calculated that he would have more chance against the Major away from Brady Castle and, in the rush, he had been able to stow away unseen in the back of one of the vehicles. Sure enough he could see the Major in one of the Land Rovers behind the police line.

"Banzai?" he enquired wistfully, pointing in the direction of the Major.

"Banzai," confirmed the Colonel with a smile, and with that we were all off again, Kabukazi in the lead and with Brendan alongside him. I had to admit that, still dressed in a kilt and wielding a vicious broadsword, well a putting iron anyway, I felt a real sense of being cheered on by long dead Scotsmen, whose ghostly outlines were running alongside us.

The sight of Kabukazi and Brendan was too much for the local police force who broke and ran for the safety of the Visitor Centre. Unsupported, the Special Branch Officers hesitated slightly before themselves making a break for cover, dragging Cumberland with them and leaving Fraser to stand alone to uphold the authority of the state.

His face flushed with excitement, MacPherson headed straight for the Sergeant, his golf club swirling over his head.

"Were you really going to lock me up, Duncan?"

"Were you really going to hit me with that thing, Angus?" The two friends laughed uproariously.

There was a sudden and prolonged outbreak of clapping coming from a coach load of Japanese tourists that had arrived, unnoticed by the combatants of on both sides. They were on a brief visit to the battlefield, during a sneak preview, prior to watching the official opening of the new Visitor Centre by the Queen the next day. They had assumed that the charge had been put on for their benefit, and their shaky grasp of Scottish History allowed them to applaud this apparent re-enactment. The loudest applause was reserved for Kabukazi, who in return bowed instinctively. Looking up he saw a group of about 40 Japanese smiling back at him and clapping enthusiastically at one of their own. Reinforcements had come at last, as he always knew they would. A strange lot he thought, not recognising the uniform. They were dressed in a mixture of red and yellow waterproof jackets and the only regimental insignia he could see was 'Nike' which was a new one on him. But he noted that each one had a camera around his neck and decided they must be some kind of reconnaissance unit ahead of the main body of troops. It had seemed like a very long time but Kabukazi knew that The Imperial Japanese Army would arrive eventually. He had been taught that the Sons of Nippon would triumph in the end, although some of these sons looked suspiciously like women.

The tourists were quite excited to be this close to the Queen, who they could see transferring to the driver's seat in one of the Land Rovers. The Major, for it was he, had watched the Highland Charge with mixed feelings. The sound of the pipes and the sight of men charging with cold steel had filled him with nostalgia. The fact that a mad Japanese Infantryman wielded the biggest chunk of cold steel was an altogether different matter. Time to make his escape and head south to the border, he decided, noting with satisfaction that the retreating former driver had kindly left the keys in the ignition. The Major regally acknowledged the cheers of the tourists as he started the engine, jerkily setting off towards the main road. Alerted by the excitement of the coach party Kabukazi watched the Major disappear with tears welling up in his eyes. Pulling himself together, he ushered the 'Photographic Unit' back on to their bus, which he then commandeered at bayonet point. In no time at all the vanguard of the Japanese Army were pursuing the Major in the direction of London. The tourists thought that they were getting real value for money on this trip and were delighted with their new tour guide, despite his peculiar archaic form of Japanese and very strange accent.

They say that in all wars, soldiers experience long periods of intense boredom interspersed with occasional periods of shocking violence. Even at major battles there were many men hardly involved at all, either because they were guarding the flanks, looking after the stores or just standing round looking at orders. The police had put down a series of checkpoints to block off the main roads, one of which was manned by PC Sargent and DS Constable. They had been there since midnight and were looking forward to a change of shift and the chance to have a cup of tea and a bacon sandwich, the first since they had started their shift.

The Major slowed down approaching the barrier, weighing up his chances of a quick dash through. He stopped at about 10 yards out, reckoning that at this distance, he would just have enough momentum to smash the pole from a standing start.

Sargent approached the Land Rover, signalling for the window to be round down.

"You can't go any further I'm afraid, madam."

"But don't you know I who I am?" asked the Major in his best regal voice.

"I don't care if you're the Queen of Sheba, you can't go past here."

The Major took out a £5 note from his pocket and brandished it at the obstructive police officer.

"Trying to bribe a police officer acting in the course of his duty is a serious offence, madam," he bridled. "Trying to bribe one with anything less than £20 is just downright offensive!"

"I have no intention of bribing you young man, this note has my face on it. Take a look."

Taking the note, PC sergeant gave it a cursory inspection. "All I can see is a picture of Florence Nightingale, and she's been dead for over a century. Now be a good dear and stop taking the mickey. Please turn around and go back the way you came."

"No, you silly man. Look at the other side."

Reluctantly as instructed, the Constable took the note, his face slowly showing signs of comprehension. "The Queen?" The policeman looked more closely at the driver; the scarf, the twin set, the tweed skirt and the wellingtons. Of course it was her Royal Highness.

"Sorry Ma'am." He stood back and saluted. "But aren't you supposed to be at Balmoral with the Prime Minister?"

"Would you want to spend a whole weekend with the Prime Minister?"

"No, I suppose not, but I will have to go and check this with HQ," and with that he moved to the side of the road talking on his personal radio.

The Major could see in his rear view mirror the bus full of Japanese tourists approaching the checkpoint. Time to go through, he thought, putting his foot on the accelerator. DS Constable, who was manning the barrier, raised it rapidly to avoid the pole as the Major powered through. Putting it down again immediately afterwards, he shook his head as the Major disappeared in the direction of Inverness. He turned round just in time to see the next vehicle, a coach heading towards him at great speed. Despite frantic waving of hands the coach made no attempt to stop. Worse still, a man at the front of the vehicle was holding what appeared to be a rifle. Constable was taking this information in when there was a flash from the coach, as one of the tourists felt obliged to capture the scene on film. This was soon followed by a whole volley of flashes in quick succession.

"Bloody Hell! They're shooting at us," he said for the benefit of his colleague, while diving into the ditch for safety. The culvert was doing a splendid job, carrying out its primary function draining the spring rain off the Culloden Moor. Sargent just had time to raise the barrier, before joining his colleague in the soggy ditch. After watching the coach flash past, Sargent climbed cautiously out of the culvert, but he and Constable were soon encouraged to take cover once again, startled to see another motley collection of vehicles careering down the hillside.

The Colonel led the next group of vehicles, anxious to catch up with the Major before he reached the main road.

His convoy roared through the open barrier and down the hill in pursuit of his father's Land Rover.

The excitement died down as these latest vehicles disappeared into the distance, leaving only the sound of faraway sheep, and the drip, drip, drip of water falling off police uniforms, to disturb the morning air.

Constable lowered the barrier again, after which he and Sargent decided to dry out, taking off their uniforms and underclothes to wring out as much of the swamp water as they could. Preoccupied with this task they were taken completely unawares by the arrival of the police convoy.

Fraser who was driving the first Land Rover, headed resolutely towards the barrier at speed. Constable and Sargent recognised Fraser immediately and, observing that Monro and Cumberland were in the back of the vehicle, did exactly what they were trained to do in such circumstances – they stood to attention and saluted. Cumberland, glancing out of the side window, observed two men, stark naked, saluting him. Even in this part of the country, inhabited by some very strange people, surely no one would be wandering around without any clothes on. Unable to believe his eyes, he decided that it must be a concussion and that he really must seek medical attention for the head. The DCI had little time to pursue this line of thought, as Fraser crashed the police vehicle through the roadblock, steering with one hand while returning his colleague's salute with the other. Unfortunately Cumberland, not wearing a seat belt, was propelled forward by the impact, smashing his forehead against the back of the front seat, instantly knocking him out once more.

Fraser drove on relentlessly, closely followed by the rest of the police convoy, though there was one straggling vehicle that appeared at the checkpoint rather late. By this time Sargent and Constable had donned their soggy clothing and seeing the lone van, were determined to stop at least this one vehicle. Otherwise their performance would not look good in their report. The van duly came to a halt as instructed, and the driver was requested to open the back doors for an inspection of the contents. PC Maclean had barely finished saying "I don't think that this is such a good idea," when a wave of dogs, excited by regaining their liberty, knocked him over before leaping up at the other two policemen. Constable and Sargent briefly glanced at each other before both decided that discretion was the better part of valour, and headed back to their watery refuge in the ditch where Maclean soon joined them. The three of them glowered on the rear bank of the ditch, as the pack of dogs bayed at them from the side of the road. Still, they thought, the others would be back soon to rescue them, but they were in for a bitter disappointment; the 'Burns Unit' was even now on its way to England in pursuit of the Jacobites. The three policemen were eventually rescued the next day, suffering from hypothermia.

The last Jacobite Rebellion had ended with the Battle of Culloden, the latest Rebellion had started with one. And the Battle was o'er and done, lost and won. As predicted, the government forces were unable to resist a charge led by a MacPherson, although the deciding factor was the assistance of the Japanese Army of Occupation in the form of Kabukazi.

MONDAY MORNING –

THE RACE FOR POWER

We eventually made our way to the Marathon starting line, or jumping off point as the Colonel called it in military terms. The whole area was thronged with people in fancy dress supposedly collecting money for charity, but in reality thriving in the publicity of wearing silly costumes on TV. While the Colonel was making a series of calls I took the opportunity to seek out breakfast. There was a whole car park full of mobile food outlets catering for every conceivable taste; amongst the obvious Burgers, Tapas, and Kebabs there were specialist outlets from every country under the sun. There was however, one notable exception – there was no Black Pudding and Bannock Cake Concession. I made a mental note to let Mrs MacPherson know so that she could sew up the market before anyone else realised.

I had a yearning for a bacon sandwich. The more that I had been denied a sandwich over the last few days the more that it became an obsession with me. In fact there was a steadily growing competition in my inner thoughts between satisfying my urge for a bacon sandwich, and my desire for carnal knowledge of Flora. Forbidden fruit indeed. As I dozed off in the night on the way south, I had a vivid fantasy of eating a bacon sandwich in one hand while caressing Flora's vibrantly nude body with the other. She took it in good spirits, however, by smearing brown sauce all over the sensitive parts of her body. After every bite of the bacon sandwich, I could add flavour with an appropriately placed lick. I was cracking up big time When I came to, I could not believe that I had had such thoughts. I don't even like brown sauce!

As I queued up I watched the giant screens showing the BBC2 televised coverage of the Marathon.

"And now, here on BBC2, we begin our coverage of the 28th London Marathon. There will be highlights on Match of the Day 2 at 10pm so, if you do not want to know the result, look away now – and for the next eight hours. And don't forget that there is still time to enter our Marathon competition – what chocolate bar is named after the Marathon? You must be over 18 and calls cost £5 per minute. If you don't get through straight away, don't hang up – Jenny at the call centre has probably just popped out to the loo. The fabulous prize for the lucky winner is two weeks in Kenya staying at a place called… um… Well, over now to Ben Hawkins and Bill Withers who will be leading our coverage today. That was embarrassing, there is no name written down on my notes, just xxxxxxx. What! We're still on air! F*ck. F*ck. And I did so well to start with, it's just not fair."

"Hello. I'm Ben Hawkins and I am joined here today by former long-distance runner Bill Withers. Good morning, Bill."

"Good morning, Ben."

"Well, it's certainly a lovely day for the 28th London Marathon."

"Lovely day, lovely day, it's a lovely day."

"I'm told that it's the seventh warmest day for the Marathon since records began. When was that... six, seven years ago?"

"That's right. This is perfect Marathon weather. There are records to be broken here today."

"Such as?"

"Well Ben, Mr. Davies of Swansea is looking to clip 10 seconds off his 14 hour personal best. I shall certainly keep an eye on that one."

"Is there any thing else we should be particularly looking out for?"

"I am very interested in the team from Kenya, who are raising funds for a name sign for their village."

"What village is that, Bill?"

"I have no idea. I think that you have missed the point Ben."

"Thank you for that, Bill. Now I think that we have Fiona down in Blackheath with some of the competitors. Are they raring to go, Fiona?"

"Absolutely Ben. I have here with me Jonathon Smith from the Sealed Knot. Tell me Jonathon, what exactly is the Sealed Knot?"

"Well Fiona, the Sealed Knot is a group of like-minded

people who re-enact the period of the Civil Wars of the 17th Century."

"Sounds very interesting, Jonathon. That explains why you are dressed up like a Pantomime villain complete with a twirly moustache. I understand that you will be carrying your traditional pikes during the race, Can you explain to the viewers what a pike is?"

"Well to put it simply the pike is a freshwater fish, greenish brown and about two feet long. It can be found in many English streams and lakes."

"And why do you carry the pike?"

"A good question, Fiona. In the days before standing armies and proper uniforms, each formation on the battlefield had to identify themselves so that they did not end up mixing it with troops from their own side. This was often done by carrying some kind of animal, or by a plant attached to their hat. Our regiment identified themselves by displaying the pike and, as supporters of the Stuart monarchy, were known as 'The King Fisher Regiment of Foote."

"Can you give us some other examples of this practice?"

"Yes, of course. Colonel Monro's regiment carried small piglets in their knapsacks, or occasionally under their arm, and were known as Munro's Pigs. Another regiment, for example, identified themselves by carrying ferrets, usually with the ferret's head sticking out above the trouser waist band."

"And what were they known as, Jonathon?"

"A bunch of complete nutters, obviously."

"I see that the pike's teeth are pretty sharp, could they be dangerous in battle?"

"Absolutely. If things were going badly in battle they could easily be used as an effective close quarter weapon. It's where the expression 'armed to the teeth' comes from."

"And how many of you are there here today?"

"There is a very good turnout. Our regiment has about 30 men and women here today, and there are other Sealed Knot regiments present."

"You said that you supported the monarchy, so will you be waving to Her Majesty as you run past?"

"That German bitch! I don't think so." And with that he marched off indignantly to rejoin his regiment. Fiona looked lost for words and, after an embarrassed silence, was rescued by the anchor presenter.

"We seem to be having some technical difficulty in transmission from Blackheath, but I can take you straight over to Greenwich where Mark Newton is talking to the Mayor of London."

"That's London," corrected the Mayor. "We've spent a fortune on that bloody logo."

"Of course. So what are your thoughts about the 28th London... um... London Marathon?"

"Good morning Mark. I am delighted to see so many people from all walks of life gathering on this wonderful occasion. As Mayor of London, nothing gives me greater pleasure than closing roads to traffic. Moving the Marathon to a Monday means that we can completely shut down Canary Wharf for the day."

Mark failed to detect the warning sign. "Can you tell us what other sporting events the Mayor's Office have lined up for us this year?"

"Yes, Mark. From next month we are going to carry the Olympic Torch from Wembley to Stratford every weekday. There will be some disruption to traffic obviously. I am also pleased to say that we have also managed to secure rights for a London Formula 1 Grand Prix. The course will take in large parts of the North and South Circulars."

"And when will that be?"

"Every Saturday, commencing in June."

"Isn't the London Marathon all about worthy causes?"

"Are you suggesting, young man, that closing roads to traffic, whenever possible, is not a worthy cause. Which newspaper do you come from, you Nazi. I'll see you never get an interview at the Town Hall ever again."

As he was dragged away by minders, the Mayor shouted over his shoulder, "Garages. There are thousands of houses all over London with garages, many of them with cars inside! I'll be introducing mini-congestion charging zones for garages. You'll see."

"This is Mark Newton, returning you to the studio."

"Well, what do you make of that Bill?"

"That's what the Marathon is all about Ben. People dressing up and generally having a good time. I appreciate a good laugh."

"No. That really was the Mayor."

"Oh dear."

"You mentioned Mr. Evans of Swansea. What other competitors will you be looking out for?"

"Well obviously, the team from the Surrey Police, Ben. I believe that there are 6 of them chained together, raising funds for police charities. We should definitely look out for them. Then there is the usual collection of Snow Whites and dwarves, characters from Star Wars, Wombles etc. And there are some serious runners out there too."

"And who should we be keeping an eye on, Bill?"

"There is Jimmy Higgins from Liverpool. He will set a sparkling pace, especially if the police team are behind him."

"Are there many other people from Liverpool on the run?"

"Yes, there are tens of thousands. Some of them might be here today at the Marathon."

"I think that the 28th London Marathon is about to start, so we are going straight over to our team at Shooters Hill."

Taking all of this in on the big screen, I had not noticed Sergeant Gordon trying to attract my attention, until I was unceremoniously hauled out of the queue just as I was getting near to the end.

"The Colonel is after you. It's time to put on our disguise."

The Colonel was indeed waiting for me and anxious to move off.

Apparently I was considered useful in my role as a Pretend Pretender. Years of planning were at stake, I gathered that MacPherson was not willing to delay the Rebellion long enough for me to slake my lust on a bacon sandwich.

"Are there you are, laddie. I have chosen a costume for you, I hope that it fits."

I was to be dressed as Jerry to match the Colonel's Tom, and to be honest I did not care what costume I was asked to wear, as long as I could get out of the kilt. Two days was more than enough to masquerade as a member of that Scottish clan, the Smiths. The costume was quite snug and substantially warmer on that clear spring morning than my previous outfit. I mentioned wistfully about the prospect of my bacon sandwich becoming a distant memory, but luckily the Colonel had brought 'rations' as he called it. I was offered a piece of cheese, which I accepted with less than good grace, and which I eked out for the rest of the day. And then we were off, the road filled with a throng of humanity, some jogging, others running, and some just walking, waving buckets and joking with the spectators.

It certainly seemed a very civilized way of mounting a coup; I wonder why no one had thought of it before. No tanks on lawns, no jet fighter planes screaming overhead, just a bustle of people, some in fancy dress, others not, all making their way in one direction, I could not identify which of the joggers were dangerous terrorists and which were there to have a good time. The two were not exclusive of course.

We had soon left Blackheath behind and were making our way to Tower Bridge where the first setback occurred. One group of Rebels from Dorset, part of the Rifles Regiment, were dressed as sheep and had made good progress until halted by an officious police officer. The policeman pointed out that only freemen of the City of London could lawfully drive sheep over London's bridges, and that no, being named Corporal Freeman did not count. The Corporal, who was dressed as Bo Peep, told his men to stop bleating about it and retrace their steps to find an alternative crossing; a difficult proposition given that they were running against the direction of flow of all the other race entrants, and the sheep were soon scattered all over South London. The Corporal spent the rest of the day trying to find them. Otherwise the whole operation was going to plan.

Some hours later we were taking a rest on the Embankment and watching the BBC2 coverage on yet another giant screen. Fiona, one of the ground reporters, was quite excited about something or other.

"There have been extraordinary scenes here, Ben. The Surrey Police Team stopped its run momentarily, to hand out fixed penalty notices to a group of young girls feeding the pigeons."

"And what happened next?"

"Well as I said, something quite extraordinary happened. A group of giant pigeons leaped out from those trees behind me. We do not know whether they were mutants, or just overfed, but they assaulted the six policemen and finally chained some to the railings. Since then the pigeons have collected 3 more policemen and have added them to the chained up group using their own handcuffs. The crowd loved it and have gone out to find some more PCs to add to the chain. Quite extraordinary."

"Extraordinary!" said Ben.

"Quite," was the response.

Cumberland had regained consciousness in St. Thomas's hospital. Ignoring the advice to rest, he had discharged himself immediately and located Monro and the rest of the team on the Embankment.

"We are going to get those bastards dead or alive," declared DCI Cumberland. His wild, staring eyes and the two plaster crosses on his forehead made him look like an unfinished game. DI Munro was sorely tempted to put another cross to finish it off, bur put the idea out of his mind.

"Now, what do we have? Any news on the Rebels, the bastards?"

"We are certain that the rebel leader is disguised as Tom and Charles Stuart is dressed as Jerry, from the cartoon series," advised Monro. We have them under surveillance over there by Somerset House."

Excited by this news the DCI insisted that they join the armed Police Team carrying out the surveillance.

PC Evans was not happy. The idea of training the policer-issue marksmen's rifle on a cat and mouse brought back extremely bad memories from the previous week. An animal lover himself, he was still having counselling to face up to the reality of what he had done. Evans was less happy when Monro turned up with the DCI. He pulled his visor down in the vain hope that he could avoid the attention of the DI who had bawled him out over the last episode. Monro had threatened to suspend Evans for dereliction of duty, but as the incident with Lawrence had never officially existed in police records, he had to relent and settle for an unofficial warning.

Tom and Jerry were pointed out to Cumberland, who then made a quick executive decision, as he strived for an image of decisiveness.

"OK, shoot them."

"We can't do that Gov," maintained Dickens. "We have been trained to issue a warning first. It's standard procedure.

"Quite right," replied Cumberland, "A warning – I was forgetting myself." On that note he picked up a loudhailer and shouted, "You can't fool me, I know who you are and I'm going to have you killed, you bastards."

Addressing Dickens he said politely, "Happy now? Now kindly shoot them." Dickens tried hard but he could not bring himself to do the deed, any more than Evans, who broke down in tears.

"For heaven's sake," exclaimed the DCI, "give me that." Cumberland snatched the rifle from him and levelled quickly. Aiming was a bit of an issue as the DCI could see two of everything, but only in hazy outline.

The first we knew about the arrival of Special Branch was the shout through the loudhailer followed by a bullet pinging its way through the Colonel's ear, his cat ear that is. What was it about Special Branch and cats? Was there a special firing range somewhere where little moggies were pegged to an overhead cable before being hauled down towards the target end, whimpering as they went? Could this be the real reason for all those pathetic notices stuck to lampposts saying 'Have you seen Tiddles – Missing since Thursday,' the owners completely unaware that Tiddles had lost out on points to Inspector 'Wild Bill' Hitchcock, in an underground facility somewhere beneath Paddington Green Police Station.

By this time Cumberland was losing it completely. His failing vision led him to take successive shots pot shots at Puss in Boots, Top Cat and Bagpuss who were jogging past. Luckily no one was injured that is apart from Cumberland, he was laid low by a pike applied vigorously to the back of his cranium. Baffled Monro looked around to see the source of this sudden rear assault, and observed the King Fisher Regiment of Foote ready for further action, pikes at the ready.

***

The Captain of the King Fisher Regiment was disappointed that his men were not allowed to carry their replica muskets into London. The butt end could be persuasive in a tight corner. The Chief Constable had personally refused permission, on the grounds that he was worried the muskets might fall into the wrong hands; he had enough troubles in South London as it was. We can only speculate why he was worried that 17th Century replica matchlocks could become the weapon of choice on the streets of Lewisham.

Gang Leader: "What the f*ck is that?"

Gang Member: "It's a kitchen knife."

Gang Leader: "The MFs don't use no blade man. We use 17th Century replica matchlocks?"

Gang Member: "But the other gangs have kitchen knives."

Gang Leader: "I don't give a f*ck what the other gangs have. We always use Matchlocks an' we're gonna continue using Matchlocks."

Gang Member: "How about a baseball bat?"

Gang Leader: "You hearing, me boy? Muskets were good enough for my father and they're damn well good enough for me."

Gang Member: "How about getting some 19th Century Brown Bess Muskets? Three times the rate of fire and less affected by damp."

Gang Leader: "Shut the f*ck up. The only Brown Bess you'll get your hands on is that pussy behind the bar at The Pike and Musket."

Gang Member: "But it put me to shame man. Only yesterday I was chasing a dude from Newham who had strayed into our neighbourhood. I carried out the 25 stage loading drill, just like you showed me, but by the time I was blowing on the match to get a light, the bastard was coming at me with one of those professional kitchen hatchets. Man, I had to run as though my life depended on it."

Gang Leader: "Dwane, I think that you might have a point. Do you know where there is a kitchen shop around here?"

Inspector 'Duggy' Bader and his men were stationed outside St Clements on the Strand, a church dedicated to the RAF, when the call came in. Jerry had been spotted on the Embankment and the sergeant and his men were to proceed south to cut him off. It had been a marvellous spring, holding out promises of a glorious summer. Young men should be out playing football or cricket, walking out with their loved ones or sitting by a lake trying to catch that elusive pike. Instead they felt compelled to do their duty whatever the cost to themselves.

"This is Squad Leader, keep formation. Close up number 6."

"Wilko, number 1."

"Don't forget that you're the tail-man, number 9. Make sure that we're not jumped from out of the sun."

"Roger, number 1."

"I say, it's a lovely day," observed number 8.

It was always like this on a mission; excited chatter from the new boys, broken up by bursts of radio static. The more experienced kept their thoughts to themselves, wondering if this was the one – the mission they would not be returning from.

"Cut the radio chatter number 8, and keep an eye out for Jerry." The squad leader hoped that his irritable message had not betrayed taut nerves and his anxiety about the impending action. He hoped and prayed that the youngsters would stick to the drill he had impressed on them time and time again. 'Youngsters'. It was only a few months ago that he also was wet behind the ears, but now it seemed a lifetime away. So many had 'gone west' already. God, he would be glad when this was all over.

"Jerry at 9 o'clock," shouted an excited number 6, "I'm going after him."

"Keep your formation… oh bugger, the daft fool's gone after him alone. Better follow him in by sections chaps, and make sure you pick up a target. Good luck and see you all back at base. Tally Ho."

"Hells bells, it's Jimmy. He's bought one – I saw him fall into the drink."

"The boys with the boats will collect him. Keep your eyes on the target. Keep in formation… watch out number 8, there's one on your tail."

"I… just… can't seem to shake him off… aaaaaaaaaaaggh! Ouch! That hurt. He's just hit me with a wet fish!"

There was mayhem on the Embankment as the boys in blue charged straight at the Royal group, shouting excitedly to each other through their police radios as they did so. The pike men of the King Fisher Regiment of Foote, even without their muskets, were more than a match for the police. Very soon a string of policemen were floating down the Thames, bobbing up and down with the waves. (Is this where the phrase 'bobbies' originated?)

Sergeant Hawkins put up a stout fight to the last until he too was cornered just south of Cleopatra's Needle. There was only one thing left to do.

"May Day, May Day. I'm ditching now." Holding his nose he joined the rest of his squad in the drink provoking a big cheer from the pike men.

The Colonel was also prepared for the surge in Police Reinforcements ordered along the Embankment towards us. Studying the original battle of Marathon in Greece, he noticed how easy it was for a small group of Rebels to hold a narrow defile against much larger numbers. A quick word to Sergeant Gordon and a small group of Rebels were immediately deployed between Somerset House and the River Thames. At the heart of the defence Tweeedledee and Tweedledum, with the line extended by three Michelin Men, four Humpty Dumpties and several Billy Bumters all with arms linked. The inflatable costumes and the padding proved to be an extensive resistance against batons, which just bounced off. Despite repeated sorties by the police they could not progress any further in the direction of Westminster until the unexpected arrival of help, hot foot from the East, via the East End. Kabukazi and his group of tourists arrived on the scene, on the trail of the Colonel, the Japanese reasoning that the Major could not be far away. The Rebels were temporarily blinded by a surge of camera flashes and failed to notice what was happening. After a surge of confidence from beating back the first few police charges, the Michelin men were suddenly deflated. There was a steady hissing noise as the effect of a Japanese bayonet on their costumes became apparent, and Kabukazi led his enthusiastic team through the gap created.

Oblivious to what was happening behind me, I was approaching the Houses of Parliament with the rest of our group. The colonel had laid his plans well and it very much looked like the operation was destined for success. I really thought that he was about to pull it off. If what he had said was true, he had only to present Charles Stuart in front of the House of Commons live on BBC2 and the Stuart Monarchy would be assured.

MacPherson anxiously checked his watch, before making a call on his mobile phone.

"What's happening? The first elements will soon reach the Houses of Parliament and there is still no sign of the King." The Colonel looked anxious as he listened to the reply.

"What do you mean, he's not coming?" The colour drained out of his face. "But who's doing this? We've bribed everyone we could think of. It can't be the farmers. They've been well paid. I've personally given money to the dockers, the fishermen, as well as customs officials, tanker drivers, postmen, hauliers, postmen, accountants, architects... everyone we could think of. I've even bribed that annoying little French politician. Who could possibly be blockading the ports?"

The Colonel listened to the reply with incredulity, his eyebrows rising in surprise. " Oh... I see. Yes. Understood." He was ashen-faced as he finished the call.

"What's happening?" asked Gordon anxiously.

"The Societe Generale des Operateurs Pedalos," was the muted reply. "I overlooked The Societe Generale des Operateurs Pedalos. What a fool I've been." The Colonel was ashen-faced.

"Who?"

"Pedalo operators. The French Government has subsidised the high fuel costs for all other forms of transport, and they feel that they have been unfairly left out."

"Pedalo operators!"

"Yes."

"You mean that they are pedalling up and down outside the channel ports stopping ferries and other boats leaving?"

"Yes, I'm afraid so. Apparently they have already forced one French Coastal Protection vessel onto the sands at Calais, outmanoeuvring the Navy boat in a deadly game of kitchen."

"Well," asked Gordon, "what shall we do?"

"Nothing else we can do. We will have to call the whole thing off and make our escape. Give the orders will you please Sergeant? Plan Scarper."

"If you're sure, Sir, but I think that the first elements are inside the House of Commons. We are very nearly there."

This was confirmed by a flash announcement on the big screen TV.

"We are now going to hear from Robin Ulster, our political correspondent, who has some breaking news."

"Thank you, Ben. Here in Westminster there is great excitement amidst reports of Wombles occupying the Commons. I can see the Speaker of the House over there and… if… I can attract his attention. Yes I have. Now tell me, Mr. Spear, these constant invasions by protesters must be giving you severe problems."

"They certainly do. We now have a tented city on the lawn protesting about Iraq, 18 people on the roof protesting about the Heathrow expansion, and 8 protesting about the state of the roof. We even have protesters protesting about the number of protests at Westminster; detracts from the aesthetic qualities of the building they say and I have to agree with them. We cannot carry on with these unexpected and ill-organised invasions. That is why I am putting forward a scheme to sell sessions to various protesting groups, paid for by sponsorship. We have had a trial run at this a week ago when we had a protest in favour of global warming sponsored by Brass Monkey Fridges!

"Yes, but what about the Wombles?"

"Wombles? This is Westminster, not Wimbledon, I think that you have come to the wrong place."

"But we have heard that a group of Wombles has occupied the floor of the house, and that Uncle Bulgaria is sitting in the Speaker's chair, your chair, even as we speak."

The Speaker scoffed at this ridiculous notion. "I think that security can deal with a few Wombles."

The Speaker was probably correct as behind the 'face to camera' pair of the Speaker and the BBC Political Correspondent could be seen Uncle Bulgaria talking agitatedly on his mobile phone as he received instructions from Sergeant Gordon. Within seconds the entire group could be observed heading to the Underground Station, presumably to catch a train for Wimbledon.

Other groups were also quietly disengaging, pushing protesting Marathon route and headed home. And that was it; the Great Adventure was over. A few brief orders from Gordon and the insurgency was abandoned. I declined to return to our vehicles with Sergeant Gordon and the Colonel. His group and several others were to overnight at a disused Army camp near Dover, before hopefully crossing the Channel the next day. Instead I decided to take a train from Charing Cross to Deal to catch up with Flora. But first I decided that must obtain some more suitable alternative clothes; I had no wish to travel in the Guard's Van with the other animals. I managed to finds a pair of flamboyant puce green fares and a tie-dyed T-shirt at a 'boutique' very near to the station; these were the only garments that remotely fitted. Julian and Sandy, the even-more-garishly dressed attendants, could not resist sending me up.

"We do not get many mice in here, do we Jules?"

"I am not surprised at these prices," I retorted and left.

Flora picked me up from Deal Station and drove us back to the Castle resigned to spending another night there. That is, only after she had managed to start her motorbike, having fallen off several times in a fit of laughter at my appearance.

Our accommodation was Spartan, our sleeping quarters little more than a whitewashed alcove in the thick Tudor walls occupied by a couple of camp beds and a small folding table. In my case, with my appearance a 'camp' bed was probably very appropriate. Still I suppose that it was good training for my likely future living quarters if Cumberland and Monro caught up with us. Perhaps I would be able to share a cell with Flora, I mused, and fell asleep with this happy thought.

TUESDAY MORNING –

FERRY PECULIAR

The interview room was exactly like those portrayed in many TV dramas, the canteen-style table, and the canteen-style chairs. It would make you wonder what the canteen looked like.

DI Munro walked in with a man who was clearly his superior and both sat down on the canteen chairs opposite to the prisoner.

"This interview commenced at 2.30am on Tuesday 14th April, 2007. Present DI Munro and Detective Chief Inspector Cumberland from Special Branch, PC Walker and the suspect."

"Look, don't you recognise me. I'm a man you can trust.'

Cumberland looked him up and down. "You know Monro, there is something familiar about him. Does he remind you of anyone?"

"Now that you mention it, he does look very much like that bastard who refused to backdate the last police pay award. But it surely it can't be him, can it?" replied Monro. "No, I don't suppose it's him. He would have resisted arrest and had to be restrained by at least six police officers using reasonable force and knuckle-dusters."

The Prime Minster went distinctly white at this thought. Monro started the interrogation while Cumberland was idly doodling on his interview room notepad.

"You have been arrested under The Prevention of Even More Terrorism Act of April 2006."

"On what grounds?"

"On the grounds that you have consorted with suspected terrorists, having items in your possession that could be used in a terrorist act, and whatever else we can come up with."

"What items?"

"Do you recognise this?"

"Yes, it looks like a list of Cabinet Members."

"For the record, the suspect has identified an annotated list of Cabinet Ministers. Is this your list, sir?"

"I don't know, they all look the same to me. Where did it come from?"

"We found it in your pockets."

"Then I assume that it is mine."

"It has your fingerprints on it."

"Then it must be mine."

"So you do not deny that it is yours?"

"Why would I?"

Monro was pleased by the way he had teased this confession out of the suspect.

"Can you explain why you were carrying around a list of prominent politicians in your pocket?"

"I was considering a Cabinet reshuffle. It passes the time."

Monro continued with his penetrating line of questioning, feeling rather pleased with himself. "I seem sir, then can you explain the remark against the name of the Home Secretary. 'Should be taken out and shot.'"

"Just a figure of speech, you know how it is."

Cumberland was doodling a very passable sketch of the current Home Secretary blindfolded and calmly smoking a cigarette, with No 10 Downing Street as the backdrop.

"And next to the Culture and Media Secretary, 'Needs a rocket under him.' And against the Deputy Prime Minister's name 'about due for a stab in the back'. And here, against the Education Secretary is, and I quote, 'poisonous rat'. How were you going to serve it, sir? Stewed at a No 10 dinner perhaps? I could go on, sir? This is very clearly a hit list of prominent politicians with details of their intended method of assassination. And what about this statement against the name of the Chancellor of the Exchequer, 'I wish that he would just disappear into a great big clunking Black Hole.' Was that a car bomb you were thinking of by any chance?"

"This is ridiculous! You can't hold me just for a few thoughts made in an idle moment."

"Oh, yes we can. We've done it before. We've arrested old men for heckling at the Labour Party Conference; we've arrested people for commemorating the names of war dead at the Cenotaph, and put people in jail for writing poems. It's nice to get hold of something juicy rather than pick on harmless people just to keep our arrest rate up. We can hold you for 42 days without trial, under the Terrorism Acts."

"But those Acts are not supposed to apply to people like me."

"Whom are they supposed to apply to then?"

"Well… you know."

"Yes, sir?"

"I mean, people with black beards… and funny names… from places like Leeds and Barnsley, not people like you and me. I'm a pretty straight kind of guy."

"Then you should not have got involved in International Terrorism sir, should you? The law is the law. It's all black and white, no shades of grey."

"Well that's not exactly the shade of colour that we had in mind. Anyway you can't keep me overnight. I know that for a fact, there's a loophole in the law you see."

"I'm afraid that particular loophole was closed this morning."

"I don't know anything about that."

"The Terrorism (Special Features) Order In Council was signed by the Prime Minister this morning. You can obtain it from Her Majesty's Stationery Office, a box set, together with Terrorist Acts I – III."

"But I'm the Prime Minister. I did not sign anything this morning."

"You were the Prime Minister. We have a new one now. Now, do you recognise this? For the record I am showing the suspect a handwritten document labelled 'B' for the records."

"Is it one of my speeches?"

"That is for you to tell me. I could read it out to you, if that would help.

"'I stand here before you as your new King. This is not a time for sound bites, but I feel the hand of history on my shoulder. This is a moment to seize. The kaleidoscope has been shaken. The pieces are in flux. Soon they will settle again. Before they do, let us reorder this world around us. A new dawn has broken, and I bring you a new style of government that seeks to restore trust in the leaders of this country. I will put an end to the idea that a Prime Minister can make all decisions in private with a small number of Ministers and advisors. In future all decisions will have to be agreed by me, your King.'"

"Shall I go on, sir?"

"Oh bugger. Look, I want to see my lawyer."

"And who would that be, sir?"

"Um… well, I suppose that it would be the Lord Chancellor."

"First Name – Lord, Second Name – Chancellor. We'll see what we can do, sir."

***

The Deputy Prime Minster had called an Emergency Cabinet Meeting. Everyone had heard the rumours and looked fairly anxious, all accept the Chancellor who appeared to be in an unusually good mood.

"Look, I've got some bad news for you," the Deputy Prime Minister said earnestly. "The PM has been caught with his fingers in the till in a manner of speaking. I'm the sort of man who calls a shovel a shovel so I'll tell it to you straight. The PM has been involved in some kind of plot to overthrow Parliament and the Royal Family."

"A coup?" asked the Home Secretary.

"Bless you," answered the Deputy Prime Minister before continuing. "The PM is now in Police Custody arrested under the Prevention of Terrorism Act One."

"Two," corrected the Home Secretary, inaccurately.

"Bless you again. We've all known the PM a long time and I think I can speak for us all when I say we hope he will be back with us soon."

"Absolutely," added the Chancellor, trying to suppress a giggle.

"Now we have to decide 'ow we're going to run the country until we know what has happening to the PM. Who's going to be in charge, that's today's issue."

"The issue," agreed the Home Secretary, nodding.

"Look 'ome Secretary. Where I come from we were taught how to use a bloomin' 'ankerchief, so I'd be grateful if we could get on without any more interruptions. Now then, it seems to me that the job of Deputy PM is to 'old the fort like. You know, when the PM is indisposed. Has anyone got anything to say about that? Chancellor, you wanted to say a few words."

It was hard to tell whether the Chancellor was grimacing or in fact struggling to avoid laughing out loud. The facial expression would, in his case, be much the same. "Thank you DPM. I do not think we need to spend much time on this. This morning I granted an audience to the Queen, and she has graciously asked me to form a new government; this I have agreed to do."

"But what about the Party?"

"I plan to hold a party at the weekend, a People's Party

and your invitations will be in the post. Well for some of you anyway. There will be fireworks, weather permitting, and of course I will have the usual celebrities performing, such as Sir Paul McCartney, Take That, and Bono and his pop group…"

"Et Tu," suggested the Foreign Minister, mischievously.

"Et Tu?" queried the Education Secretary.

"Bloody 'ell! Now there's an epidemic We'll 'ave to 'ave the place fumigated to get rid of any bugs."

"I think that he means U2, Deputy Prime Minister." The new PM fully intended to remove all unwanted bugs in a Cabinet Reshuffle, starting with the Foreign Minister. "Now if there is no further business, I have to get on and run the country."

"Shouldn't we have an election?"

"We will have an election when the voters realise who has really been responsible for the fantastic economic success that we are having, and realise that TB was only basking in reflected glory. I will continue to make sound finance the hallmark of my administration. After all we don't want the Queen to be worrying about her pension, do we?"

"And what about the Prime Minister?" asked the Foreign Secretary.

"Ex-Prime Minister. I have consulted the Lord Chancellor, who tells me that just because someone has broken the law we don't have to prosecute him if it is not in the country's interest to do so. That is, if the government does not want any murky secrets coming out. But I'm afraid he will have to remain in prison until I have considered the matter."

"And how long will this take? And then what will we do with him?"

"I think that to examine all the issues properly will take a while. To consider the pros and the cons, and to decide what is in the national interest will take me, oh let me see… about 42 days should do it. I am sure that he will meet a lot of old friends inside jail. And after that, I was thinking of, maybe, a high profile ambassador's job, a peace envoy perhaps."

"How about Special Ambassador to the Middle East?"

"Thank you Home Secretary. We are clearly thinking along the same lines. But I thought that we could start in a small way with say, Special Ambassador to the Gaza Strip and see how that tumbles out. Now if there is no more business I have to be officially sworn in by Sir David Frost and then meet the Leader of the Opposition, Sir John Humphry."

***

The ferries were running again after the French Government had sent in the crack Legion de Lilos, a sort of low cost Special Boat Service who had been rushed to the Channel Ports from their bases on Corsica. It was, in fact, the largest sea battle that the French had engaged in since the Battle of Trafalgar, and fought in much the same way; opposing fleets in line ahead engaging in broadsides before boarding parties moved in to finish the job. Trained to work in two-man teams and using high-powered water pistols, the Legion soon overpowered the Pedalo operators in the early hours of Tuesday morning. The Legion had perfected counter-insurgency techniques and knew exactly which combination of inflatable whales, crocodiles, turtles and dolphins to use in any particular situation. It was a textbook operation, although some members of the opposition later claimed that the Government Troops had been a bit too heavy-handed using their inflatable truncheons.

Flora and I had managed to book a passage on the 11am ferry, and we were glad to be on our way to Calais, her motorbike stowed below. I had bought us both a cup of coffee and we had sat down to watch Sky news. Sitting on a boat, looking at Sky with Flora Macdonald had a certain historical resonance and, I thought, a certain inevitably from the first. I kept expecting a Director to shout 'cut' at any moment. There was news about the attempted Rebellion, but with a twist. A screen said that the Chancellor of the Exchequer would make a public announcement in five minutes, and that programmes would be delayed. The usual marshall music was being played to underline the gravity of the situation but interspersed with tracks from Take That and, bizarrely, Sir Paul McCartney singing the 'Frog Song.'

The talking head of the Chancellor duly appeared.

"Good morning. Most of you know me as the Chancellor of the Exchequer, but I am now appearing before you as Prime Minister. Her Majesty summoned me to the Palace this morning and asked me to form a government. In the interests of the Nation, and despite my own lack of personal ambition in this area I have, with a heavy heart, acceded to Her Majesty's request."

The screen switched to pictures of a motor cavalcade driving through the gates of Buckingham Palace. The guards in the sentry boxes stood smartly to attention as the convoy drove through. I had heard that, as a mark of honour, the Gurkha Regiment were now allowed to take a turn on sentry duty, their distinctive green uniforms and puttees contrasting with the bright red tunics and Busbies of the Coldstream Guards. This particular Gurkha had bottle lens glasses and reminded me of Kabukazi, but then they all looked alike to me. The screen moved on to scenes of the Queen, dressed in a blue formal dress and with the sash and the Badge of the Garter, greeting the Chancellor. As the camera closed in I could see that the Queen looked nervous and bit wild-eyed, no doubt recovering from the ordeal of being kidnapped. There was another possible explanation.

'But that's not the Queen, it's… it's the Major," exclaimed Flora.

We both looked on open-mouthed as the Major formally greeted the Chancellor on the steps of the Palace before going inside.

I should have guessed. It was Kabukazi on guard duty, no doubt in the hope of assassinating the Major, when taking the Corgis for a walk. Kabukazi was probably armed with pocketfuls of black pudding to attract the dogs, and with them their owner, for this very purpose.

As always Flora looked on the bright side. "Perhaps we could get a Royal Pardon. We should ask my Great Uncle before he is found out."

We had several more cups of coffee, watching the events unfurl in London on the television... The announcement in Parliament, the crowds in the street cheering, the potential cabinet members to-ing and fro-ing to No 10, some looking pleased and others suggesting that they had always welcomed the challenge of going to Northern Ireland as a Minister. There was no word from the outgoing PM who apparently was still helping the Police with their enquiries, although later it had been announced that he had been taken to hospital following self-inflicted injuries which the six policeman standing nearby were unable to prevent.

Eventually nature called and I set off to the men's heads, as I believe they are called onboard a ship. There were several big parties of nuns on board and I assumed that there must be some major religious festival in France, or perhaps they were all on their way to Lourdes. This made the boat fairly crowded particularly as there was a backlog from the day before. I eventually managed to force my way to the toilets. I automatically choose the far end of the group of three urinals, thinking about male vanity as I relieved myself, staring at the wall ahead. A Dutch Professor had carried out tests with urinals and had discovered that men never stood next to each other to urinate if given the choice. Confronted by a group of three urinals, two men would almost inevitably choose to stand at either end. And so it was no surprise that, when the door opened, the incoming nun choose to stand at the far end. I was mentally congratulating the Dutch Professor for this invaluable insight to male human behaviour, and wondering what the female equivalent might be when the penny dropped. The nun's face was strangely familiar, particularly with the cigar clamped firmly between the teeth, nestling under an insect Maginot line of a moustache.

"I see you that made it, laddie," said the Colonel, "and I trust that you have Flora with you."

"I do Sir, safe and sound. Did you see the Major on TV?"

"Aye, I did. Lets hope that it's a while before they discover the truth."

"Do you think that the Chancellor, I mean the new Prime Minister, suspects?"

"I am sure that the new Prime Minister has found it all very convenient. He has the Queen, I mean the Major, under virtual house arrest, supposedly for security reasons. I doubt that anyone will get very close to our new Monarch for a very long time. And he has the former Prime Minister under lock and key; I think that we have all been had. We thought that we were outwitting the authorities, but it seems that they were manipulating us all the time. I should have known that Special Branch would only have sent Cumberland and Monro, the two most incompetent policemen I have ever come across, so that we would not be stopped in our plan to kidnap the Heads of State. We played right into the hands of an evil genius in the heart of government."

"You mean the new Prime Minister?"

"Yes, I think he planned it all. Even down to the protest of the Pedalo operators. You have to hand it to him; I suspect that he was one step ahead of us all the way, why else would he have allowed Laurel and Hardy to be put in charge of the Counter Terrorist effort? But at least we succeeded in changing the Monarch, and for a Scottish one at that. We also have a Scottish Prime Minister as a bonus," the Colonel laughed uproariously, which had the effect of creating a spray inside the ship. "But I have learnt one thing, apart from never trust the French of course. I know now why the Major is so keen on dressing up in women's clothes. The feel of the silk, the nylons… you should try it some time," and with that he was off.

"Well, if the Major is carrying out Royal engagements, what has happened to the Queen?"

"The Prime Minister came with us, to London, but I think that the Queen was left at Castle Brady. So I suppose that she must still be there."

***

Mrs McGregor called into the Laundry Room to see how the Queen was managing the ironing. "You seem to be getting on quite well, Mrs Windsor."

"Thank you, Mrs McGregor. One was doing awfully well to start with but now the machine seems to have got a bit bored and doesn't want to work with me any more."

The Housekeeper cast an expert eye over the equipment and soon came up with a solution. "You need to put some more water into the iron, Ma'am, through this little nozzle here."

"How clever of you. Oh, there's so much to learn. Do call

me Liz, no one ever does. Are you sure there is no one I need to meet? One of those interminable foreign ambassadors presenting their credentials perhaps, usually lot of fuss over nothing. None of them seem to have anything worth presenting, although there was once an Italian diplomat hung like a donkey… Oh, where was I."

"You don't have to see anyone Liz. Just finish the ironing and then we can put our feet up, and have a nice cup of tea and a chat."

"And I don't have to make a speech, or sign any documents?"

"No love. I tell you what, perhaps I can show you how to make bannock cakes later."

"Do you know, Mrs McG? I feel so much at home here, and you have been so kind – a friend, even. I don't think that I want to go back to being Queen. Do you think that they will miss me? Will I have to go back?"

Mrs McGregor put her arm round her new friend. Mrs Windsor was great fun, no task was too small and every task was carried out with almost childlike enthusiasm. And it was good to have someone else to talk to, as the place seemed lifeless since all the men had gone; even Kabukazi had seemingly disappeared into thin air. "Well Liz. I don't care if they do want you back, I won't tell anyone you're here if you don't. You can be assistant housekeeper, if you want."

"One is so grateful Mrs McGregor, may I call you Janet?"

"Certainly Liz, now hurry up with the ironing. If we can get that done and the bannock cakes baked, we'll have time to go down to the Crown and Usurper for half of Guinness and a wee dram each before dinner."

215

TUESDAY AFTERNOON –

'BONNIE' PRINCE CHARLES
AND CLYDE

Flora had managed to find us a room at a Gite somewhere
south of Paris. We were heading for her family villa in the
Cote D'Azur but obviously would not be able to make it
there in what was left of the day.

With her passable French she had managed to persuade
the Patron that we were quite harmless, and this was despite
the fact that we had turned up out of the blue with no
luggage of any sort. Flora's infectious good humour was
carrying me along, but somehow I did not think that our
host was entirely convinced that we were not fugitives from
the law. We were allocated an outbuilding that was clearly
once an animal shed, but it had been refurbished to such
a good standard that I was looking forward to a peaceful
night. I was exhausted from the events of the last few days
and suggested to Flora that perhaps we should retire to

bed early to catch up with our sleep. She was amenable to the suggestion and added that a bit of Doctors and Nurses might be appropriate before I passed into never-neverland, a thought that had clearly not crossed my mind. Before that she had to make some phone calls about the villa and check that the bike was tuned up, ready for the next day. She promised that we would create our very own Act of Union at seven minutes past five – that is at 17.07, the year of the Act of Parliament. Was our lifetime together to be governed by some weird and wonderful Jacobite Clock I wondered? Obviously it would continue to be dinner at 19.46. What other anniversaries was I supposed to commemorate, lunchtime at 13.14, the Anniversary of Bannockburn? Still I wasn't going to argue, I was on a promise. My only concern was that something would come up before then, not only what I hoped would be coming up, but some unforeseen event that would leave me frustrated once more.

It was not an ordinary raid. Details had been carefully co-ordinated between *Paris Match*, *Le Figaro* and Canal Plus TV. At the agreed signal the local Police chief, Inspector Cloulesse, raised his loudhailer.

"Attendez. C'est le Police. C'est votre cinq heures appel de reveil."

Drawing the curtains slightly to one side, I peered briefly through the window. I had just enough time to note the semicircle of blue-clad interior police surrounding the front of the building before a hail of small arms fire peppered the front of the barn, smashing windows and taking great wooden chunks out of the front door. Now I knew how Lawrence had felt. Had the British Government issued instructions to kill me on sight? All I ever did, for heaven's sake, was to impersonate a giant mouse. Surely an ASBO would have been sufficient. I made it to the back door running out into Flora's anxious arms. She had the foresight to start the motorbike engine, the sound being concealed by the noise of the pistol fusillade.

Inspector Cloulesse was doubly surprised. He had not been told that there was a back door and was stunned when our motorcycle roared round the corner of the barn, scattering the police who were busy reloading. He was even more surprised that neither us fitted the description of 'Les Moto Vole Amoureuse' who had been responsible for a number of armed robberies of Supermarkets in the area, a latter day Bonnie and Clyde. The Patron had failed to mention that neither of us have dark skins nor that Flora had a shock of red hair and a face full of freckles. We passed so close to the Inspector, that he could have counted them in detail, as he watched open-mouthed in astonishment while at the same time signalling his men to hold their fire. We left the Gite without paying, it seemed the right thing to do in the circumstances, and were soon back on the motorway. So much for the promise! I had hoped for something hot and throbbing between my legs but had not anticipated that this would be Flora's motorbike. C'est la vie!

***

It was a year to the day that we had arrived in France. I had managed to obtain a teaching post at the local university while Flora had helped out at the local Library; that is until she took maternity leave. At the moment she was out in the garden with our young son Charles, or 'Pretend Pretender Junior', who had had the good grace to enter the world on the 242nd Anniversary of the Battle of Culloden.

I was passing the time watching the Major on Sky News, who was at that moment opening a new investment bank headquarters in Canary Wharf. The Major was of course convinced that he was inspecting bomb damage from the blitz, and this led to some confusing conversations. His talk about frequent raids, with more to come, had frightened the bank staff into piling into the lifts en masse. Eager to return to their desks, they set about removing or destroying incriminating documents as fast as they could. This had to be done urgently before the FSA regulators or worse, the police, turned up on the scene. Ironically the bank went bust a month later along with several more banks and financial service companies. So, in a way, the Major was indeed surveying the financial wreckage of Docklands, which was completely 'bombed out' by the end of the following week. There would be heart-rending scenes of people carrying away their precious possessions in cardboard boxes; all that was left of their once secure lives. The Major organised soup kitchens to provide at least some warm food to carry the poor souls through the night. These proved to be very popular after the wine bars had shut, and were the source of many complaints from the local kebab shops. And the Major was seen to be visibly moved, on camera, when he visited the hundreds of people taking refuge from bombing in the Jubilee Line underground stations. (The tube drivers' wildcat strike was resolved shortly afterwards – Editor).

On seeing the Major going about his regal duties every day, Kabukazi had finally realised the gross error of his ways. The Major had been a woman all along, and was only pretending to be a man. His family honour, which he had thought had been horribly besmirched, was in fact intact. Kabukazi took exceptional pride in his new role as head of grounds security at Buckingham Palace, taking turns at sentry duty and occasionally jumping out from behind bushes at night scaring the living daylights out of any *Sun* journalist researching lax security at Royal residences. He had become such a major tourist attraction in his own right, that the times of his scheduled sentry box duties were reported in the Japanese national newspapers.

Flora had kept up with the news from home, using the Tartan Codebook that she had hung onto through thick and thin. She was delighted to learn that the Queen, now known as Mrs Windsor, was the new Housekeeper at Castle Brady following the retirement of Mrs McGregor. The two friends were often seen together at the Crown and Usurper, or staggering back in a fit of un-ladylike giggles. Sergeant Fraser was currently on the High Moor with the latest Chief Constable, hot on the trail of a major bird's egg thief, and the Reverend Rabbie Kray was facing a run off for the post of Convenor. Kray seemed to be extremely confident; his opponent was unavailable for comment, or pretty much anything else really – he had not been seen, or heard, since Pinky and Perky paid a visit to pledge their support to him in person.

Cumberland had become an artist of some renown and some of his early doodles were now fetching tens of thousands of pounds. I was quite pleased about this as I had a complete series of doodles on Lawrence, which I had managed to pick up cheaply at a gallery in Nice before Cumberland's fame had spread. I thought that I should keep these in memoriam but with the sudden rise in value, they also constituted my pension fund. Monro was still on the fast-track with the Transport Police on the West Coast line, this being the only job he could get after the Rebellion. Sergeant Constable had been demoted to being an ordinary PC and PC Sargent had been promoted to Sergeant. Everyone involved in Special Branch thought that this was a sensible solution to a continuing problem, all apart from PC Constable of course; he would now have to be the back end of any future pantomime horse.

The Colonel had been delighted to hear that the government had quietly dropped any charges against the persons involved in the attempted coup. The Attorney General had decided that it was not in the National Interest to proceed further, but vehemently denied the comments that the government had anything to hide or that there was any kind cover-up. He was now free to return to Scotland together with the rest of his 'lads and lassies' many of whom were with him in Zurich. I suppose we all were.

The Prime Minister was involved in yet another relaunch of his image. He had had more relaunches than the Weymouth Lifeboat, which was also regularly sent out to save men in distress. The former Prime Minister was currently negotiating the supply of building materials to some of the residents in the Gaza Strip. He would give them the pile of bricks currently supporting his 4X4, if they would return the wheels.

I had yet to meet Charles Stuart, the descendant of Bonnie Prince Charlie and the genuine Pretender. He was currently running an upmarket Paris restaurant, 'The Restoration', with his good friends Alex Romanov and Napoleon Bonaparte. Flora had invited them all down to stay for Pretend Pretend Junior's christening, where we were to be joined by the Colonel and a few of the others. Napoleon apparently had a plan that he wanted to talk to us about. The Colonel also had a new plan, which he said he would explain to us when he arrived. I have very mixed feelings about this. From my routine round trudging off to Guildford University and coming home to domestic disputes with Lawrence the cat, I had become one of England's most wanted men. I had spent a confusing week not really knowing what was happening around me, generally in somebody else's trousers or, even worse, in somebody else's kilt. And, then, having fled the country of my birth, I had become a target for some French Police who had obviously watched *Butch Cassidy and the Sundance Kid* too many times. And every other day, I seemed to be a pillion passenger relying on Flora to get me out of trouble. In retrospect I had the time of my life – and all of it with Flora.

I really couldn't have asked for more.

THE HISTORICAL BACKGROUND
THE JACOBITE REBELLIONS

The Romans had been sensible people; they had built a wall, an early form of passport control, between that part of Britannia we call Scotland, and the proper bit to the south. The Anglo-Norman Monarchs were less pragmatic and insisted that they should control the whole island, even those bits where heather was considered to be a delicacy. The struggle raged to and fro for centuries, with sometimes the Scots pushing the English back past Hadrian's Wall, and sometimes with the English Lording it in the Scottish lowlands. From time to time, in their spare time, the English would also campaign in Ireland and Wales until these two countries were also considered to be part of English Crown. It was doubly galling therefore that it was not safe for the English to go too far north of Edinburgh even with an army, just in case they met a bigger one.

Eventually the English came up with a masterstroke, they would make the King of Scotland the King of England as well. He could hardly wage war on himself. And so it was that in 1603, James VI of Scotland became James I of England in a sort of two-for-one deal. By this time the lowland Scots were mostly domesticated, but even James Twofer had great difficulty in ruling the Highlands and Islands, which were still populated by hardy Clansmen 'without a shew of civilitie'. In 1625 James died, and was succeeded by his son Charles I, thereby establishing the Stuart dynasty as the rightful monarchs of England and Ireland, as well as Scotland. Charles managed to get by with just one number, although, as he often pointed out, it was 'Numero Uno'. Unfortunately Charles was carried away by his own self-importance and managed to upset both the Scots and the English; the Scots by insisting on the introduction of the Book of English Prayer north of the border, and the English through taxation and for ruling without a Parliament. We know the resulting conflicts as the 'English Civil Wars' although the people at the sharp end were usually Scots or Irish. Eventually, it was agreed that Charles' head should be chopped off so that he could not come up with any more bright ideas; and everyone would then be happy. Unfortunately, the dictator Oliver Cromwell and the Commonwealth replaced Charles and being happy was made illegal. Cromwell is mostly remembered for his two excellent ideas of banning Christmas celebrations and opening up the West Indies for tourism.

When, on Cromwell's death, the post of 'Numero Uno' again became vacant, Parliament appointed Charles' son, Charles II, as a new King. Charles II knew how to be happy and, although not everyone could afford several mistresses at a time, the Restoration was a time of great jollity and fun; apart for those people who had ventured to the West Indies, they generally died of swamp fever.

Charles was followed by his own son, James II. Somehow James could never get used to the idea that he was only number II and believed wholeheartedly in the Divine Right of Kings. He failed to realise that there were some matters he should not tamper with, i.e. food and religion. James had spent much of his childhood in France under the protection of the French King Louis XIV, and had come back to England full of peculiar ideas. Apart from the delusion that French cooking was superior to our own, he had also decided that the French religion was much to be preferred. People had only just become used to being Protestants and had no desire to change back again and, as a result, James II was overthrown and fled to exile in France, the traditional bolthole for Stuarts in trouble. There then broke out the war of the Three Kingdoms, the first of the Jacobite Rebellions. The three Kingdoms concerned were England, Ireland and Scotland although Dutch and French troops and ships were involved, the Dutch because the latest Monarch was William of Orange who had married Mary the oldest daughter of James II, both sound Protestants, and the French because they were at war with William and the Dutch in the Low Countries. The Scots and that Irish were fighting to restore James to the throne but, despite a number of victories, eventually gave up in despair.

Finally Parliament decided that, after the death of Anne Stuart, the other of James' daughters, no Stuart would ever again become Monarch and passed the Act of Settlement in 1701. Parliament stipulated that in future the House of Hanover would provide the hereditary Kings and Queens of England and Scotland. As George, the current Elector of Hanover, was thought to be a bit of a rural bonehead who spoke no English, and anyway would probably spend most of his time abroad, it was hoped that Parliament would not be troubled by again by Monarchs with bright ideas. If George did have any, Parliament could always pretend that they couldn't understand what he was saying. When the Scottish Parliament maintained their right to appoint their own Monarch they were quickly encouraged to abolish themselves through a mixture of threats and bribes, a decision which was ratified by the creation of the United Kingdom of Great Britain, with one Monarch, one Army, one Flag, and one Parliament. This Act of Union was passed in 1707, but the abolition of an independent Scottish Monarchy was to only to take effect on the death of Anne, the last of a chain of Scottish Monarchs stretching back nine hundred years, longer even than the English crown could boast.

Queen Anne died in 1714, and George Ludwig van Braunschweig-Luneburg was proclaimed King of the United Kingdom and Ireland. This was too much of a mouthful for some Scots to pronounce, and quickly declared their support for James II's son, James III, who with his father had lived in France and Italy, constantly stirring up trouble in Scotland with armed expeditions, and never giving up hope of restoring the Stuarts as joint monarchs, or at least to restore an independent Scottish Crown. He was known in England as the 'Old Pretender'. As each Jacobite revolt came to nothing, the baton was passed to James III's son, Charles Edward Stuart, also known as Bonnie Prince Charlie or, by the English as the 'Young Pretender'. In 1745 Charles Stuart raised his standard in Scotland and was quickly offered support by many of the clan chiefs, picking up further support as he marched way south. After the Scottish army had inflicted a string of defeats on the British Forces, the government brought back seasoned professional troops from Germany, led by George II's second son, the Duke of Cumberland. Forced back into the Highlands, the Scots finally stood at bay at Culloden, close to Inverness where, on 16th April 1746, they were decisively defeated. After moping around the Highlands and Islands for some weeks, presumably living on a diet of heather, bannock cake and black pudding, Bonnie Prince Charlie sailed for the island of Skye, helped by local girl Flora Macdonald. With further help from Cluny MacPherson and others, the Prince finally managed to sail back to France, and into romantic history.

There were no more Jacobite Rebellions after that, until recently that is.